A
BOX OF
CHOCOLATES

A book of poems

by

Sonali Deuskar Gurpur

Published by
Z's Publishing Company LLC
zspublishingcompany.com

DEDICATION

To my family, with love.

EPIGRAPH

"My Mama always said life was like a box of chocolates. You never know what you're gonna get,"

Forrest Gump

CONTENTS

PROLOGUE

Dear Reader,

I present to you **A Box of Chocolates**. Every one of these delectables has been carefully handcrafted. Some are plain, some are very sweet, a few are very bitter, some have an ooey-gooey center inside, some are nutty, and some have the kick of adult-ish liqueurs in them. **A Box of Chocolates** is my journal in a longish prose poem. Each individual poem is a chapter within the monolith. Anything that caught my attention that day would end up as a journal entry in garbled language, some call it poetry, so I could get it off my chest and go on with my life.

This is by no means entirely autobiographical. I took stories from family folklore, the neighborhood news rag, the national dailies, conversations overheard in parking lots, alumni get-together updates, letters from home, mythologies, movies, fiction, history lessons for my kids, songs on the radio, dreams, musings, meditations ... and made them go to work as "journal entries". Together, they describe an archetypal journey. The first section is about my current obsession with HUMAN CAPITAL. May I brag? This poem was quoted by someone very important in a very important setting. The next section is about the integration of ANIMA and ANIMUS. Reflections on childhood, children, and parenting are in WHEN WE WERE VERY YOUNG. I WENT TO THE ANIMAL FAIR is a collection of metaphorical poems about critters. EKPHRASIS is self-explanatory. THE EVOLUTION OF EVE is a zero to shero story. MIDNIGHT TRAIN TO DORKISTAN is a feminine point of view on the evolution of Adam. Perhaps I should've named it THE EVOLUTION OF ADAM but I don't feel qualified to accurately describe that archetypal journey so I stuck with friendly ribbing. The EPILOGUE circles back to HUMAN CAPITAL.

In the text, which also works as a treasure hunt, are many allusions to other texts, movies, and songs that conjure up a world much larger than my humble words could ever hope to, left to their own devices. It's mostly in English, with a sprinkling of Hindi, because the theater of my mind is eighty-nine percent Hollywood and eleven and four-fifths of a percent Bollywood now. I'm a bit of a 'chaser of light' so the interplay of 'light' and 'darkness' figures prominently in my writing.

The interpretation of the larger story depends hugely on the individual. Each character or situation does double duty at least. The text holds meaning for the music buff, movie fan, cultural historian, geographer, language arts teacher, parent, and child, in different ways.

It is simply a message of hope and, hopefully, it reads like one.

Best,
Sonali

HUMAN CAPITAL

"...The profound and the profane have always come to me holding hands..."
(Missing Ingredient)

i. "Krishna" by Sweta Shrivastava Saxena (Saxena©, Krishna)

1 Human Capital

What dark god would they be praying to
those who play Cronus or Kans or Herod devouring their young?
Where goes the image of motherly love and femininity
when you are reminded of Lilith?

What happens when cultures devour their own future?
Do you end up with lost cities in the sky?
Is that all?
Consider what else is lost.

Why must we wait and still do nothing
when gas chambers are being built,
poppy seeds are being sown,
children are being sold?

What if we stopped selling ourselves short?
What if we refused the executioner within?
What if we refused to remain numb?

It's easier said than done.

2 Movement

What constitutes a movement?
Is it the turning of galaxies,
the turning of colors in autumn,
a shapeshifter changing direction,
a demagogue tweaking a single word
just so?

Is it the polar and grizzly hybrid at the melting pole?
Is it the flight of the monarchs over thousands of miles?
Would you call the guillotine and the Gutenberg movements?
Is it a movement if you move from tribalism to collectivism?
Is it the subtle shift of the "I" at the center of your universe
to "We"?

ii. Cricket Match by Prafula Shukla (Shukla©)

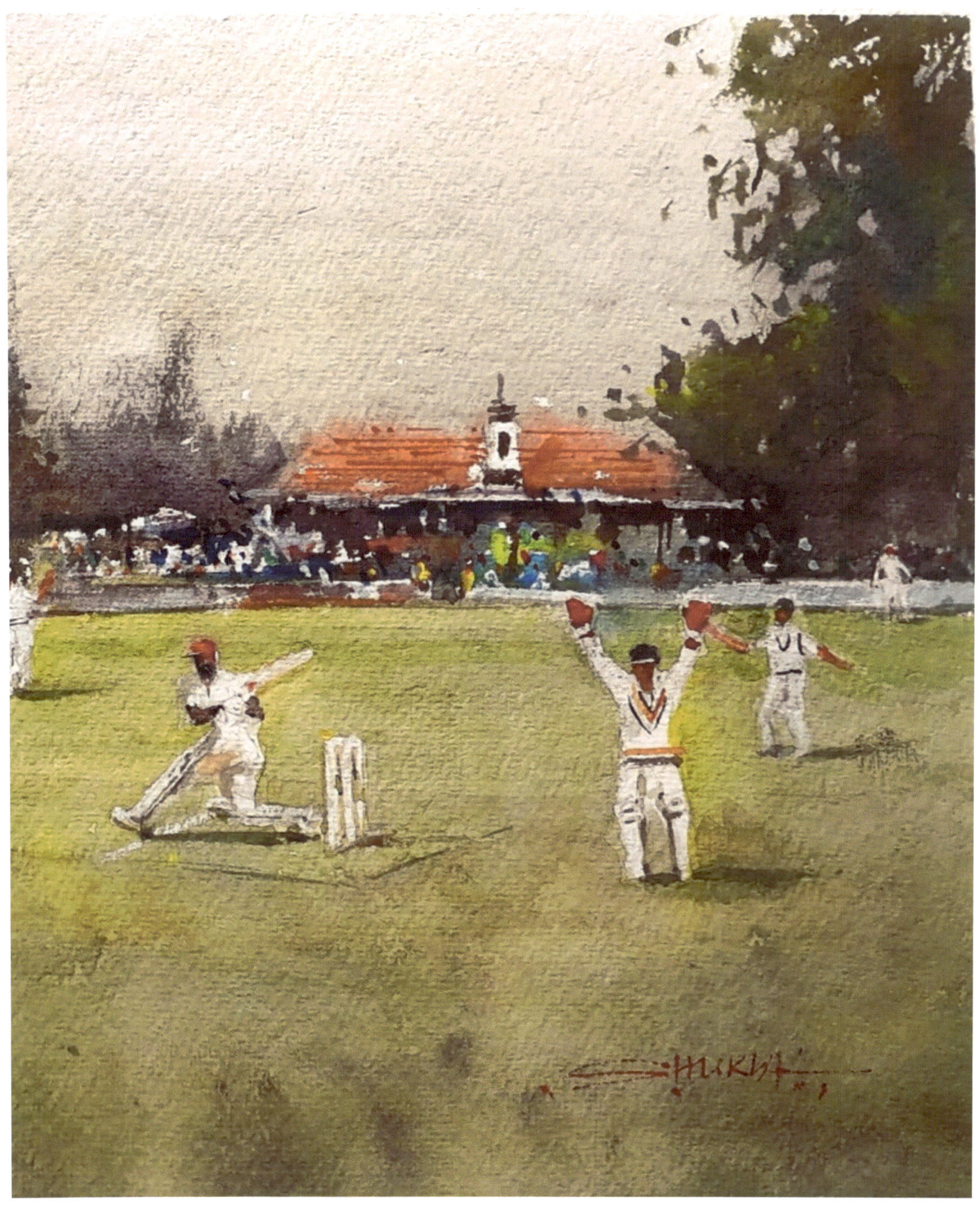

3 Colonial Cousins

I was walking along Folly Beach in Charleston, South Carolina.
the song playing in my head was Sweet Caroline,
inspired by the state name, I guess.
I was walking off lunch:
American chop suey and apple pork.
It had been prepared exactly the way I had eaten it as a child,
in a restaurant called Nanking in Hyderabad.
I was misty-eyed from nostalgia,
thinking of all the great times
my family had around the dinner table
at the Chinese restaurants in town.
We were regulars at Blue Diamond, Haiking, and Nanking.
I knew what pretty much everything on the menu tasted like.
This food felt like childhood with my cousins in the long summers
in Hyderabad.

During lunch, I just had to say it:
I said, "I'll bet you the cook's Indian."
My husband thought that was hilarious.
When the waitress came by to refill our glasses,
he told her.
She turned to me looking amazed,
"Wow! The cook is from India.
How did you know?"
I said, "I just knew from the way the sauce tastes;
it tastes like smoke-filled rooms in Chinese restaurants
in my hometown"

Just as we finished lunch,
a Chinese gentleman came by and said hello.
He was the chef,
and he was so happy to meet us.
We spoke for a while.
His family had lived in Mumbai for years,
he went to school somewhere in Colaba,
his extended family was spread all over India
in cities I had visited.
I had probably eaten in their restaurants.
And here we met, foreigners in a new land,
bonding over Indo-Chinese cuisine

that has no parallel in this world.
We both like the fish in Mumbai better,
and complain about how the kids have no clue
how good mangoes taste.
He asks my husband what he does,
and he says half his family is in software too.
He knows all about SEEPZ.
They chat about the booming IT industry in the area.

As we left the restaurant, I felt like I had just met family.
All Asians are very similar people even if we don't all look alike.
We meet and we're talking about our kids, and our cousins,
and which grocery store had the best litchis last summer.

And people speak of migration like it's something new.
It's not.

I've met expats with accents exactly like mine,
who were expats from other places before.
There was a job search counselor whose family lived in Malabar Hills, Mumbai.
His grandparents had left Europe in search of a safer place in the 1930s.
There was the girl with golden hair whose parents are foreign correspondents
living in Chennai.
She misses idlis with sambhar, and so do I.
We'd met at the Udipi restaurant in Atlanta.
She missed going for kutcheris,
she loved to go to Golden Beach,
she missed the fragrance of jasmine garlands.
I was like, yup, yup, yup, girl,
I know how that feels.

I look around at my neighborhood and think sometimes
my South African neighbor,
my Pakistani friend, and I
are always exchanging notes
on where to find the best tea, Chutney, and Cadbury ...

And cricket! Ah, cricket!!
We relive the grand old days of childhood,
reminding each other of our top five favorite matches ever
and we all agree Kapil Dev, Imran Khan, and Dennis Lillee
were the best pacers.
They were magicians to our young eyes.

We didn't exactly know what sleight of hand had occurred
until we watched the action replay
and listened intently to the expert commentator's report.
Our South African friend is especially fond of batting averages.
Viv Richards and Sachin Tendulkar are her heroes.

Funny where we find our heroes,
my Pakistani friend thinks of Imran as her hometown hero
from Worcestershire where she had lived during her school years
after her family immigrated to the UK from Rawalpindi.
That really ticked off her grandma she says, laughing uncontrollably.
The old lady would remind her Imran was Pathan and not British,
and mutter under her breath, "Iskander de pooth firangi ho gaye."

Did you know the Chinese also sing "Auld Lang Syne"
followed by "Clementine" every New Year's Eve?
A Chinese friend once told me that.
I said to her I had no clue our early lives
on either side of the mighty Himalayas
had been so similar for years.
We discussed that at length,
and she said "Clementine" was a Spanish song
that got translated into English.
I reckoned that probably happened
during colonial times in the USA.
It probably traveled to Asia
with the British troops that left in the late 1700s.

Music and food!
They keep us tied to our complicated histories.

Tell me again
why we hate immigrants
when we are all a group of cousins
related by history, language, religion, culture, humanity...

4 Borderlines

Blurring lines on an antiquated map-
maps of the mind, of mindsets,
maps of languages, and trade routes,
national borders going in and out of style,
mood swings of the geopolitical timeline
of recorded history.

We never learn our lessons,
lessons found in every history book.
Footprints on the sands of time
state loud and clear
what we deny, we empower.
Therefore, the guillotine awaits the tyrant.

5 It's the Spirit of the Enterprise

Why do we romanticize hunters, and not butchers, or taxidermists?
Fishermen too, especially the loners who catch the biggest fish?
What is it that our primitive brains recognize as skill and courage
that a butcher cannot deliver?
I guess it's akin to the adulation we profess for a Prithviraj or a Lochinvar,
as opposed to a pimp, no matter how vast his brothel.

Robber barons, for all their wealth, are seldom invited to share their wisdom
in public spaces and in places of learning or worship.
They need extreme machinations to get their word out if they ever do.
Over time, I guess, they realize no one cares about what they think or feel.
People instinctively guess their motives are simple and primitive,
and so must be their minds, so why bother seeking them out for their knowledge?

It is a rare human being who perhaps started out a Cain,
sees within himself his brother and knows he is his brother's keeper.
He plunges into the deepest, darkest waters of his subconscious,
a minesweeper, he sweeps away everything
that prevents him from being a wholesome person,
akin to an Akbar when he found the Buddha, Jesus, Allah, and Ram,
and finds there's room at the table for a prodigal son.

6 Breathe Life Into Me

It takes a village

Welcome city slicker to my abysmal little village.
We're nothing special, we're just another village,
like Asterix and Obelix's generic Gaulish village,
or Hansel and Gretel's non-specific Germanic village,
or Balraam and Krishna's Gokul, an average Indian village.

Have you ever watched an ironmonger at work?
When the iron leaves the forge it is malleable,
hot, tender to the touch that shapes it.
Watch how it glows and then goes dark.

Ever watched a potter's wheel until you got dizzy?
Here's to you, you thing of clay,
spinning on an axis not of your choosing
until your new identity has been assigned to you.
You are going into the fire soon
for your Creator to finish the job he started.

That's our watering hole.
The cook's a rough man
with a menu of rough meats and rough potatoes.
Medium-rare is not my favorite kind of steak,
I like mine well-done,
but he's been thinking I'm ready to be trimmed and served
with a side of lettuce and garlicky rice.

That's where we buy everything for the home,
lightbulbs, cradles, ladles, and all.
The carpenter had time on his hands
and started to whittle
into what he had thought was a job well done,
a finished product,
an ornate headboard.
With every nick of the chisel, he took away what didn't belong
with the frieze of roses and acanthus leaves he had dreamed of.
He has yet to burnish the wood.
Splinters remain attached to his creation.

If you look along the outer wall of the old courtyard,
there's a little plant growing in the dust.
The gardener had seen that the vine was dying
and set out to resurrect the languishing little plant.
He pruned and watered and applied every effort
the man at the garden shop told him to.
Two green leaves and a dried-up tendril is all we see at the moment.

The Lord have mercy on unfinished projects.
They really could go either way.
How do you city folk deal with your unfinished projects?

7 The Apprentice

I, Abecedarian,
holding a tiny spark in the wind,
await my master's return
down the ladder.
He, the lamplighter,
I, his student,
we've done this for an hour.

I've watched him shimmy up the ladder,
trim the wick, wipe the glass,
pour the oil, light the lamp,
in one surefire sweep.
I stand below
in awe,
the former village idiotess.

My master wheezes,
he is unwell.
He's blown his lamp out with a gigantic sneeze,
and I offer him the dying flame
I'm holding on to for dear life,
and he refuses it.

"Go on lassie,
you'd climb the ladder
better than this old fool".
He believes he's said it all and he leaves.

"If he be a fool
who be I?
A fool's fool?"

I take a quivering step,
ladder in my wake,
another quaking step
into the unknown,
the dark,
the murky,
terra incognita.

8 Warp & Weft

I bring the brimful of *"yes"* and *"no"*
to my lips and taste the bittersweet fire.
Oh, I've had some before,
before I knew what was in it,
before I ever knew what it would do to me
or does to anybody.
You see, I was tricked.
Anyhow, each of us carries a flaskful
hidden from prying eyes.
When asked we refuse to admit
any knowledge of the substance.
What is this elixir?
This flagrant bouquet?
Who makes this stuff,
and to what end?
Why won't it ♫ *quench my desire?* ♫
This must be some sick cosmic joke
because I sniff a conspiracy of the gods.
It smells like roses, as always,
and gives me a heartache when I've had some.
I'm tired of this game.
Go away!
Vex me no more,
and let me tell you,
if I find no reason to tell
little white lies like I was told,
I might start dropping hints
to the uninitiated about this,
this thing that makes me
weak and strong,
laugh and cry,
sing and die,
all at once.

9 Missing Ingredient

The profound and the profane
have always come to me holding hands.

For all these years I've welcomed the profound
into the crucible of my life,
and dealt with the profane by ignoring it,
then berating it,
then ridiculing it.

With each supercilious thought and action
I lost something I couldn't identify.
It felt like life sometimes, sometimes like love,
and I never could tell which was the case.

I hadn't known I was to alchemize the pair of them
to hear the punch line to The Cosmic Joke.

10 The Water Bearer

The Magi have their gifts,
the Saki her wine,
the dancer her tambourine,
the nightingale her song,
the rose her blush.
Why must I
walk about secretly sobbing
while I pour water
from my half-filled pitcher
into imperfect receptacles?
My gift is no nectar,
no song sublime.
Why does it hurt so much
to pour fresh water
and hope
one day
it will turn into love?

11 Leaky Cauldron in the Sky

There's a big brew-ha-ha
over a magic potion in a magic cauldron in the sky.
When poured into your cup it will spill over,
staining your lips, your fingertips, your very spirit.
Everything you touch will giggle and squirm
with childish glee and wonderment.

This alchemy of love in action
sends shooting stars into the unseen realms,
a meteor shower,
that burns through the darkness,
that burns up deadwood on contact,
in an easy-to-miss smolder.

We're lucky the cauldron leaks a little.
If you can find the drip and hold your cup just so,
you can catch the elixir *drip drop drip splash.*
You don't have to be seated at the table of Zeus
and have Aquarius serve you from his pitcher.
You can be mortal and drink moon drops fallen from the sky.

You will get drunk and everything will become very very funny.

12 The Wishing Well

A penny tossed into the dark rippling waters,
magnified,
it shimmers
momentarily,
like a restless goldfish but it isn't one.

What magic is life
that that which lives
and that which doesn't
can never seem alike forever?

The waters stand still.

13 Pixel

Moving dots on this piece of glass
have made contact
with the chemicals in the brain.
Nothing is as it seems.
Much has been lost in translation
between the virtual and the temporal,
most of all humanity.

14 Matchless Wonder

We the people have

burned trains in protest,

burned bras in protest,

burned our boats,

burned bridges,

burned brides,

burned witches,

burned saints,

burned our own lands

in scorched earth policies,

burned our brethren with napalm,

burned books we didn't understand,

burned our leaders in effigy,

burned ourselves in fits of madness,

burned spontaneously as oddities,

burned evidence that proved our guilt,

burned memories that we couldn't deal with.

What's left?

15 What Ails Thee?

The blue light from the television screen underscores care packages.
Pamphlets rain down from Chinooks.
The plastic wrap comes off the packages and the goodies are a welcome relief.
The loose-leaf papers fly away on a summer's breeze.

The business of living must go on past these few weeks.
Pain and hunger return.

What now, dear benefactor,
now that the band-aid's soiled and the painkiller's worn off?

Gifts of blankets, teddy bears, and t-shirts
must always be accompanied by shipments of seed, sod, tractors, and such.
And how about prefab homes, moisture farms, and solar panels?

16 A Force of Nature

The stars scatter on us all the same amount of sparkle.
Rain drenches us all the same.
Love comes looking for us all at inconvenient moments.
The sun warms us all equally,
and yet only the meek shall inherit the earth.

17 Thingamajig

Thingamajig:
That's what Maneesha called herself.
Of course, she didn't tell anyone that.
That was her new term of endearment,
or jokey nickname for herself.

It was her son's favorite new word.
He hadn't yet discovered "whatchamacallit".
He would soon, and then "doohickey",
but she had grown attached to "Thingamajig".

She felt like a product of disintegration, a "detritus",
an amorphousness so without definition
she couldn't tell where she ended and where the world began,
but still very useful and more resourceful than ever before.
So, she stuck with Thingamajig.

Always a logophile,
she found out that a "salmagundi"
is an unorganized collection or mixture of various things.
So is a "farrago",
but there was too much "salamander" and "gundi" in there,
and "farrago" was too close to "Fargo" and "virago".

Her varied hobbies and roles in life
drew her to "omnium-gatherum" but that was too pompous
for something she saw as more a "crazy quilt" than a "smorgasbord".

She wasn't terribly sure about "crazy quilt" either.
"Quilt" yes, "crazy" no.
She was saner than the circus she traveled with.

She thought a "pastiche"
of responsibilities, roles, talents, and hobbies was she,
but a pastiche just sits there and does nothing,
so Thingamajig was she.

By and by the little pieces of the puzzle she was
began to recombine in surprising ways.

For a while, a set of skills would come together
and serve as a response to a new responsibility.

When she outgrew the role
some of those skills would go on ice,
some would wither and die,
some would grow and constellate
into a new pattern of being and doing.

Sometimes she could systematize her talents and character traits.
Often, she couldn't hierarchize her roles and responsibilities.

Thingamajig has been through several
refurbishments, upgrades, and revamps,
but she hasn't told anybody yet
she sees herself as Thingamajig 10.2.

18 Quantum Leap

My energy levels are strange.
I can do nothing, and yet
I feel I ought to spin the world on my fingertip.
Where do I go from here?

"Jump," I hear,
"JUMP !!" I hear again.
I'm so startled I jump without thinking.
3-Gs hit me, and I hear a crush.
I land.

I love it here.
Just as I am beginning to think,
everyone understands,
I feel daggers in my back,
Lotsadaggers.
Friend and foe alike have chosen
to wound me.

For forty years I have turned around
and offered my jugular as well,
this time around I will keep on keeping on.
If you want to be my friend,
jump.

19 Second Banana

Abbott and Costello.
Hitler and Goring.
Freud and Jung.
Bush and Quayle.
You get the point.

There's a place for seconds in this world,
a place the seconds scoff at,
and yet sometimes wear like a badge of honor,
and sometimes escape to better things.

What would it take for you to step out of the shadows
and deal with the spotlight?

There will be epithets.
Usurper, if it were sudden.
Whore, if you are young and female,
especially if you look good in a dress.
Witch, if you are older and respectable.
Gay, if you are young, attractive, and male.
Madman, if you are older, decisive, and male.

There's no getting away from that.

Remember the little Slumdog covered in poo?
Mr. Bachchan saw nothing wrong with him.
It was those with time on their hands
and no laurels to rest on who created all the fuss.

Merlin knows Arthur is to be found somewhere hereabouts,
humble, attentive, quick, worthy of the destiny he must fulfill.

20 Rags to Riches

"If you got free by any strange behavior,
more power to ya."
Consider this.
I had a torrid affair with the blank page,
and it saved my life.

I think I was in the tabloids for weeks
in four different languages,
but that's a small price to pay
for freedom.

The whole thing began
as a last will and testament
scrawled out on a piece of paper,
a bucket list awaiting the approval
of a lawyer and friend,
with an abysmal feeling
of having but a handful of years to live.

The breath raspier each day,
spoke of leaving in a year or three.
With what little was left of my time,
I thought it would be best
to just set free the souls around me.
As I saw it,
a few words could accomplish that.

The last rush of the Life Force
I imagined was my ally of the moment.
I could see clearly now
what wrong I had done,
and I had the foresight of one
who has nothing to lose.

By the time the ball I'd set rolling
struck down nine pins in all,
I'd be obsolete,
dead as a Dodo.
The sympathy wave would
wash away the awkwardness of the scenario.

I wonder who said it first,
"Laughter is the best medicine."
They forgot it is food too,
food for the soul,
for if you don't laugh for a few years,
you will surely die.

Out of the blue
broke a cosmic joke
and set me free,
free to laugh.

Funny what people can think
when they haven't heard you laugh in years.
They think you've lost your mind,
or they are very, very threatened
by your happiness,
which they perceive as your "strange behavior".

Then there are those who insist
they can't deal with your depression,
nor your paranoia,
when you've only just
understood why it matters to them
that you remain in chains,
in a million little pieces,
a puddle on the floor,
a sick puppy fighting for its life.

So apparently, you're so sick in their eyes,
they think you'd be better off dead,
or so they proceed to insinuate.
Beware! Their every word is a lie.

"What cages? What chains?
What pieces and what puppies?" you ask.
Somewhere along the way
a veil of darkness had fallen away.

iii. If you got free (htt2)

Suddenly I could see
into another dimension
and knew there were cages
of hate, fear, guilt, gold, ivory, lies,
that needed to be unlocked.

Having been set free unexpectedly,
I believed I needed in a hurry
to do the same for my brethren.

Yes, out of the cages,
there is danger and love,
laughter and life,
censure and acknowledgment,
happiness and strife,
but it still is freedom.

And would you believe it?
Friends will tell you at such a time in your life,
what you really need, really, really need
is a two-week-long affair.

I turned that around in my head
for two seconds and knew
there was some faulty logic right there.
I had no need to possess anyone for two weeks,
no need to mess up
what was right for those I love.

Solomon's judgment was uppermost in my mind,
simple yet profound,
if you love someone
you wouldn't allow for them
to be battered, butchered, bagged, and bought.
But it has been suggested
telling fools, they're fools
is in bad taste.
So, I let them make their
various suggestions
to see which one was the wildest.

Propelled by the most unusual of circumstances,
I began to see cause and effect differently.
Beliefs long held as truths receded
giving up space to a new way of seeing.
"Symbolic sight" I hear is what they call
this strange animal.

Then I had the wildest idea of all.
I'd have an affair,
longer than two weeks,
much, much longer,
with the blank page.

So, I laid down emotionally naked on the blank page
and turned into a Diane Warren song.
It held me close a long, long time.
Love, the dork side, and the dark side,
all put together in this potboiler
turned into a symbolic Fourth of July for the spirit,
an ensign of fireworks and freedom.
Now how that happened
is a mystery to me.

Just an aside, in case it should matter to you,
if jumping off cliffs,
or jumping out of cakes,
or jumping out of dark corners in dark alleys
is not your forte,
don't worry,
you'll get the hang of it.
And please don't question
the logic behind actions such as the aforementioned.

I no longer question
the power of love to heal,
or think to question
if such profound love exists.

21 Feeding the Fury

iv. Photograph by Sonali Deuskar Gurpur

I have a gut feeling,
that this chocolate cake will quell my hunger.

C-H-O-C-O-L-A-T-E C-A-K-E

What's not to love about it?
Decadent, rich, awe-inspiring.

It will humble the enemy within
the fury, the foe, that rises within
periodically
from long suspended animation.

The enemy does not know about my new secret weapon,
Sleek, quick-acting, potent chocolate cake.
I smirk then my eyes glaze over.

CAKE ATTACK

The fury lies immobilized.
Perhaps it is dead.
Perhaps it is only playing dead.
What if, a little later, it rears its ugly head again?

I'm out of cake,
and who cares about later?
I'm happy now.

22 Lotophagi

There are some of us who cannot stand on two feet like the homo erectus
because we are the lotophagi.

We cannot think, act, speak, nor live according to our wishes,
but we do the master's bidding who feeds us the lotophagi.

We've bartered our souls a little at a time and unwittingly given a little
of the body and the mind each time as a package deal of the lotophagi.

We see pictures of street children sleeping on footpaths,
of Mumbai or Kolkata or Hyderabad and we're looking at us, the lotophagi.

Numbed beyond human suffering, our codes of conduct are not
those that serve our best interests or those of our offspring.
We're as broken as the lotophagi.

It is time to reimagine the scenario.
The lotus sutra proves it is not the lotus that is evil, it is those who misuse it.
The gullible, vulnerable, and faithful dupes are the lotophagi.

Look that captor in the eye, let the light of your soul shine
through your brokenness, and say, *"I am no longer enslaved."*

23 The Emancipation Proclamation of the Body-Mind-Soul

Two souls hang in golden scales,
in perfect balance,
he The Body, she The Mind.

It wasn't always so.
Once upon a happy time,
they were honored for who they truly are,

BodyMindSoul,
yin and yang,
a unity.

Then his mind
became maddened,
then saddened.

Her body was sold into slavery,
but her mind they couldn't shackle,
so it lived, somewhat.

Reassurance came to him
only when he was
The Body.

His ultra fine mind
was damned with faint praise
and constant ribbing.

Her body was disrespected,
pushed to the limits,
and her capabilities questioned every day.

Somewhere along this treacherous path
idealism, self-worth, and vision
were eroded.

A thousand miles
through the desert,
they walked shod in sandals.

Rats will gnaw at your feet when you sleep,
vampires will swoop in when you bleed,
to drool upon a potential feast.

The evil ones may have their evil designs,
but there is a certain something
that they cannot kill.

Atlas shrugged,
causing a seismic shift in awareness,
and they remembered being whole once.

They took back their souls,
they took back their minds,
and their bodies too.

They put them back together,
piece by intricate piece.
They're happy now.

ANIMA ANIMUS

"... river wends its way through destiny, doership, drenched in rose and musk"
(The Awful Simplicity of Ten)

v. Painting by Debjit Paul (PAUL©)

1 A Thousand Pardons for I Know Not Who I Am

They say Radha was born blind with two lotuses for eyes.
She was healed when Krishna looked in her cradle
and she saw for the first time everything she had ever wanted to see.

This story is so sweet, I am compelled to imagine
what the baby girl might have thought of it.

Perhaps she thought, because as you know she didn't really know,
that she was made of a thousand lotuses that brimmed with life,
and brimmed with nectar, and brimmed with light.

2 Desert Rose

I walked through the desert,
with no shoes and no shawl,
looking for you.
Don't turn me away now.

I offered you my soul
again, and again, and again,
and all you ever did was ask,
"Do I know you?"

vi. Digital Art by Fatima (Fatima©)

3 The Accidental Cubist

This poem is a retelling of the story "The Little Prince"
by Antoine de Saint-Exupéry

Her eyes on one shard,
her voice on another.
That was his reality.

When he was lucky
there'd be a touch of color
replacing the sepia of his memories.

The brokenness amused him
by becoming a kaleidoscope
when he turned his head this way and that.

But there still were
a million little pieces
he'd have to collate in his mind.

He walked through the desert
and accidentally stepped on a rose crushing it to pieces.
The air filled with a sweet perfume.

Further away, way down the road
his misfortune was to step on a snake that
bit him on the ankle making him comatose.

Slipping in and out of venom-induced sleep
he frothed at the mouth and felt helpless,
angry, and weak as never before.

The sun grew hotter and scorched his skin.
Thirst played games with his mind
on a terrain where mirages are commonplace.

Unexpectedly,
slipped the veil of the *purdah nashin* before his eyes,
and nothing was the same anymore.
The world had healed seamlessly.

4 The Colors! The Color!

One drop of sunlight
warm, yellow, sweet, stark, honest,
I had caught in the hollow of my hand
as the casket closed upon me,
an eggshell,
that stayed dark for years.

It was dark but unbeknownst to all, fertile.
One fine day a crack appeared in the shell.
Out stepped the ingenue,
into a technicolor world.

5 Why Women Should Stay Home to Raise Their Young and Why Men Must Never Go Whaling

Because they come back with fish stories
and those about the one who got away.
If they went to Brokeback Mountain
they come back with no fish at all.

And Ishmael was just following
a great big sperm whale
called Moby Dick
through the great big
vast unknowns of brine
when he was really looking
for a freshwater stream
with a divining rod
that took him places
he'd never gone before.
And he got lost
trying to find himself.

vii. A Photography By Zac Peckler (Peckler©)

6 The Erroneous Theory of Venus' Envy

It is such errant nonsense
that Venus is not happy
the way she is.

The only little whiff of
a half-joke-mock-complaint
I've ever heard from her
is that
she thinks
it's not fair
Adonis has a weathervane
and divining rod and she doesn't,
"I'd love to be able to tell
which way the wind is blowing
or where to find fresh water
with so little effort
any given time of day."

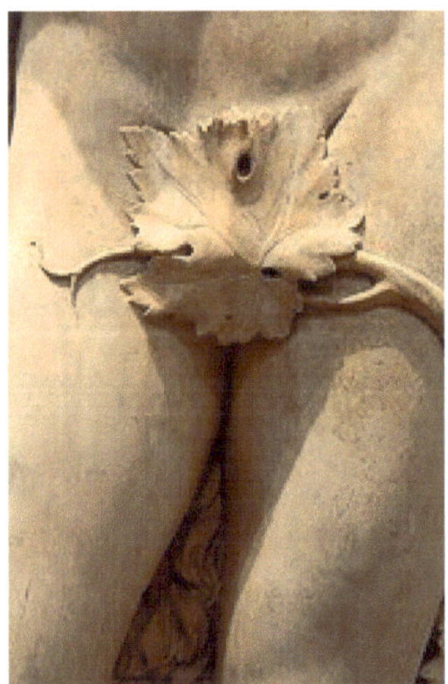

viii. A Photography By Zac Peckler (Peckler©)

7 The Deafening Sound of Silence

Sorry I screamed so loud,
I mean I'm glad you came to see me.
I screamed because I thought I'd die if I didn't.
Well, I screamed without thinking really.
I thought I'd die if I didn't see you.
How many miles did you walk to see me?
It must've been a million,
and all you saw were my tears.
I wish I could hear you,
but I can't for this thick wall of glass between us,
longer than The Great Wall of China.
I hope you can stay
but I'll understand if you must leave.
I'll go away with no answers.
It grows dark even as we speak,
so you wouldn't know I'm smiling now.
I am.
That deafening sound of silence gives way to
a deepening sound.
It is indigo,
a benign vortex,
pure, silky, luminescent,
God-like,
like the ripples on a placid lake
impinged upon by a single pebble,
the closest thing to a softly whispered secret.
Did you hear that?
A hum.
Om.
And now the door's closed I suppose.
I hear nothing, again,
but I don't feel helpless anymore.

8 Cupid's Wet Wings

ix. Gulmohar tree (Sethi ©)

For twenty years I have watched the trajectories
of the lives of two friends
I love dearly.

Those lifelines were to intersect momentarily,
then loop themselves around the globe,
never to meet again.

I remember when I saw them for the first time
matter-of-factly sharing *jhaalmuri* out of a newspaper cone
under a *gulmohar* tree at the bus stop.

I thought I saw a match made in heaven,
but apparently not,
and had wished for something like that for moi.

I hear from them both on birthdays, Diwalis, some January firsts,
and the occasional *"I-just-called-to-say-hello"* days.
I've watched them grow closer separately.

When I called her yesterday, she was reading *"Kafka on the Shore"*.
Of course, I couldn't tell her he was all caught up
in the *"Windup Bird"* book.

They never ask of one another so I never know if I should tell.
Earthly duties come above the flimsy emotions
of the disobedient heart.

Speaking of earthly duties, she told me she had cooked *Ven Pongal* rice
with Tellicherry peppercorns. He'd been complaining about airline food
a few hours before and asked if *dal bhaath* was too much to ask for.

I suppose it is quite impossible for the pair of them to meet for brunch,
one on an airplane going six hours south from Beijing,
the other in Winnipeg snowed in for the weekend.

What could've gone awry at the time their fates were drawn?
A GPS malfunction in high places? A Y1K catastrophe for
a complete lack of software engineers, what?

Last year in May they left the kids in *Dida*'s care,
and vacationed in Paris to celebrate twenty years together,
he and *Boudi*.

Her grandmother passed away the same week and she flew to her hometown
changing planes at Charles De Gaulle at eleven there, or so said my Caller ID.
He left a little after three as I saw on the photos he emailed me.

He's becoming more spiritual, he says. His kids say, *"Baba's getting old,*
he's turned vegetarian, the smoking's gone for good, he even stopped to pray at the
bodhi tree after having driven past it hundreds of times that we've seen."

He does not know she was there last year,
right across the street at the hospice where she was born,
to pick up a copy of her birth certificate.

"Who am I," I ask myself, *"to play Cupid twenty years too late?"*
I would've sooner, had I known how deeply marked these two lives
would become on account of a summer fascination of 1985.

That summer, he says, he flew on wings.
I suspect if she hadn't brought with her gifts of anger and a false sense of security,
he might never have crashed.

It used to bother me that he'd say he's bored and tired of it all.
"It's all getting too old, and too easy, but it's a living…"
words no one had ever heard from him before.

I know, heartless as it might seem, that in the crashing, burning,
then forging anew his sense of who he really is, he found his true calling,
loss of ennui, and that million-wattage smile.

She tells me she can't get through one summer without reflecting
on the exact shade of orange that was the *gulmohar* in the breeze,
so she's simply resolved to stop remembering.

She said she'll plant narcissus outside the window to admire next April,
when like the still-frozen earth,
she feels only half alive.

Feelings turn into thoughts, thoughts into words, and words turn to naught.
For whose amusement do we speak our lines on this stage called "The World"
when it all stops to make sense?

9 More Than Meets the Eye

"Hadd ho gayi hai goondagardi ki. Cartoon banake khada kar diya hai shareef logon ko."
~ Rajiv (Akshay Kumar in WELCOME, 2007)

My homage to Stephen Sondheim's "Into the Woods" and T.S. Eliot's "Wasteland"

PART I

A funny thing happened on the way to the movies that night.
I was late and running in high heels,
and you were running away from the opening credits.
We met mid-flight at the bottom of the stairs,
going in contrary directions.

If you hadn't seen me and stopped
I'd have run into you and fallen to the floor,
completely embarrassing myself.
But embarrass myself I did,
by trying to dodge you
and failing three times,
making the exact same mistake
all those three times
and thinking you must think,
"What a klutz!"

All I saw of you were your shoes,
perhaps not as clean as
you'd have liked them to be,
but I knew in that instant
I already knew the wearer
of those shoes,
and liked the wearer too.

A feeling of peace took over me,
the closest I've ever felt
to this thing people call *"World Peace."*
Even to this day
I've seldom felt any peace that closely
approximates that beautiful feeling.

Our paths crossed again
in a stone-cold empty library
where I combed the stack of encyclopedias
looking up differences between
voiced fricatives and voiceless affricates.
But you didn't have studying
on your mind, did you?
You followed me there, didn't you?

Now I've always believed
there's a time and a place for everything.
How was I to ever know
what else other than reading
could ever happen in a library?
Imagine that!

What imagination you have!

And the persuasion skills
of Mighty Joe Young in the wild.
Cues were missed, signals crossed,
lost in translation
between man speak and woman speak.
I thought you needed new shoes,
and was I wrong!

Then you charmed my mother
until she believed you're
the nicest boy she'd ever met.
I suspect she loved you
as much as the son she'd always wanted.
You must've found out very quickly
I didn't tell her
about your little misadventure,
if that's what you had wanted to know.

PART II

In the blink of an eye
more than meets the eye
unfolded.

As I see it now,
archetypes fleshed out and came to life.
Boy met Girl.
Pepe Le Pew knew that he knew that he knew.
The inner Wolf espied the inner Lamb,
both equally surprised and thrilled,
vaguely aware this was meant to be,
they borrowed a little archetypal fur
from one another and stuck it to their own
like lovers will keep a lock of each other's hair.

To stretch the metaphor a bit more
I bring up the possibility of Red Riding Hood
having heard the Call of the Wild,
and point to Jason questing for The Golden Fleece.
♫ *And Mary had a little lamb whose fleece was white as snow* ♫

BTW in this version of RRH,
RRH wouldn't say to the Wolf,
"What big eyes you have, Grandma"
and the rest of the spiel.
Instead, she'd offer, *"What a fertile imagination
you have, Mr. Wolf, and, oh my, what big feet!"*

But then, that's not how the story went.
Thence began the damage,
to the brain, to the heart,
and almost nearly to the soul,
and a bit some to the bodymind,
all on account of the wolf feeling
plenty underappreciated and unloved
as did RRH.

The Lamb made an unconscious decision
to stay 30 feet or more
away from the Wolf at all times,
lest he make her howl,
and get her in a lot of trouble
alongside him.

Neither were wordsmiths nor strategists
back when they were locked in their own wordlessness
and innocent misery.

The Fates connived against their youthful frailties.

PART III

The shoes, the shoes!
I crave your patience for shoes and foot fetishes,
for right about then Cinderella lost her slipper
and cringed every time the Prince tried to put it back on her foot.
She fled and hid behind some lame excuse,
while her brain turned to sawdust
and her heart to mush.

Briar Rose ran in bared feet through the forest
and walked right into Phillip.

The sparks that flew about
at these inadvertent meetings started up a smolder,
then a brushfire,
and then a raging inferno.
"When engulfed in flames, make no decision"
had been drilled into their impressionable minds,
and they predictably obeyed.
In fact, they had been schooled in the axiom,
"Under no circumstances make a decision."
It wouldn't be for years that
they'd hear Saul bellow at them:
"What are you doing under the circumstances?
Get out from under and you get on top!"
and the Fates would concur.

Despite it all, this story grew feet
and traveled a long, long way from where it started.
Tongues wagged in heads that knew
but part of the story.
A gentle breeze,
and some third millennium technology,
carried the snippets around
in convoluted paths,
until one fine day
there were just enough pieces
to pull together a comprehensible collage
of timeless shape-shifting archetypes --

Shiva and Shakti,
Rapunzel and The King's Son,
Eric and Ariel,
Cupid and Psyche,
Shakuntala and Dushyanth,
Othello and Desdemona,
and they all had ♫ *had a bad day*♫

007 had lost the Spy Games to a little girl.
The Beast had finally alienated Beauty for good.
Shakti, as Sati, had flung herself into the sacrificial fire
and sent Shiva into a cosmic rage.
The Little Mermaid was not so little anymore.
Rapunzel had cut off her locks in exasperation
and even lost her singing voice.
Goldilocks had lost her equanimity.
Ophelia was dead.
♫ *Desperado*♫ had drawn the queen of diamonds.
The Snow Queen was fresh out of snow.
Cruella had married Roger Dear.
Mr. Incredible, though appearance would deceive, felt off-kilter.
All was out of whack.

Aye, there's more to this than meets the eye.
There are goings-on that'll open up your third eye.
Beware!

PART IV

So, who won?
Tom or Jerry?
The Coyote or the Roadrunner?
Fuddy Duddy or Bugs?
It doesn't matter who won or who lost.
It's about chasing a dream,
the thrill of the hunt,
the skillful fabrication of the colorful exaggerations
extolling the many virtues of the one who got away.

Sometimes getting too close to your one goal,
meaning you have no other,
is like flying too close to the sun.

And before I forget
Cupid's arrow left a wound
from where we bled love everywhere we went.
Then, his evil twin,
his Dark Shadow,
struck with an arrow tinged with poison.
What won, Love or Poison?
Go figure!

PART V

Anima and Animus fell madly in love.
Shakti had split into Me, Myself, and I,
Prakriti-Durga-Gauri,
Mother-Warrior-Consort
and reintegrated,
resplendent, purified, aglow in feminine energy.

Shiva showed up on Shivratri.
When she touched his feet asking him for his blessing
she saw him again in a beautiful explosion of divine light,
the bluest, purest, most comforting light she'd ever seen.

The fountain of youth had been visited.
♫ *Hum pe hairaan hai teer Sikandar ka*
Hum pe kurbaan hai neel samandar ka ♫
Joie de vivre coursed red through our veins.
Anima and Animus were wed.

10 Why Worry?

When all is said and done,
Love remains unspoken.

When all the pros and cons have been looked at,
Love goes unnoticed.

When all is analyzed and accounted for,
Love remains unwritten.

When love and hate lock step,
Love comes out ahead.

x. Multimedia Illustrated by Jahin Hasin Nishi (Nishi ©, Ashima, 2023)

11 Microtransactions

Ashima, the Zamindar's wife, all of twenty-three,
married for five years now to the oldest son of a middling estate somewhat past its prime, was expecting
their first baby and feeling very large and cumbersome.

The Zamindar, Ashima, and the Zamindar's brother waited
in the drawing-room for the Rani Sahiba to emerge from her living quarters,
ready to go to the movies with her family, a matinee.

Rani Sahiba, now widowed and mainly uninvolved in the daily workings of her estate,
had taken to social work and gin rummy, not an uncommon combination of pastimes among the ladies of
her generation, in her neck of the woods, if they had been born into wealth, or had married it.

"It's too hot" said the Zamindar's wife, fanning herself with a magazine,
"especially for a whale as large as myself. I should be swimming in the oceans."
She had a faraway look in her eyes, a look her husband never understood,
nor dared to address.

Her devar chuckled and said, *"Boudi, you are such an imaginative creature,
you should write! I'm sure you'll tell your kids the best stories ever,
the kind Darwan used to tell us when we were kids.
He spun them fresh as he drawled in Bundeli."*
The Zamindar nodded and shook his head in the same gesture,
a 'yea and nay nod' peculiar to our part of the globe, that no other nation on this large blue planet has
mastered or fathomed yet.

xi. Painting by Pramod Kurlekar (Kurlekar ©, 2012)

"Fatso, make me a cup of tea," said the Zamindar pointing at his wife with his chin,
a rather unremarkable and unimpressive chin, superseded by thin lips, and a Brylcreemed mustache.

His wife started to wiggle her very pregnant body to the edge of her seat in an attempt
to get out of it. The Zamindar's voice droned in her direction, in an Oxbridge Indian accent, *"You have gotten
so lazy, you haven't made me breakfast in months.
My mother made my scrambled eggs this morning because the cook didn't show up.
At least make me tea."*

The Zamindar's brother blanched a little as he spoke, *"Dada, every time Boudi goes into the kitchen these days, she
runs out the backdoor almost immediately and throws up behind the hedge, don't you know? Boudi, relax, I'll make us tea.
Ramu left for Begusarai early this morning to attend his sister's husband's funeral. The poor man died of cholera. I told Ramu
he will be quarantined for three weeks when he returns. Jamini cooked lunch today."*
With that, he sped toward the inner rooms to get to the rasoi a hallway
and a verandah away.

The Zamindar's wife finally spoke, *"No wonder the jhol was so good today, not the oily mess Ramu prepares. I overate.
Poor man, I hope his sister will be okay. Perhaps we should employ her. Let me talk to Ma,"* said the Zamindar's wife,
and her husband rose from his chair,
glaring.
"I say what happens here. My mother is a nobody. I own the estate."
His wife cringed as he spoke, and for the next fifteen minutes she couldn't bring herself to look away from
the tiny black stain on the rug that had proven impossible to wash out every year on rug washing day.

xii. Painting by Gail McCormack (McCormack ©)

The Zamindar's brother returned with a tray laden with goodies, a teapot, and teacups nesting awkwardly due to the delicate handles that protruded. They were finely crafted, but not designed to fit well together.

He put the tray down on the ottoman.
Rani Sahiba called out to them from the hallway,
"Sorry darlings, let's go. I was on the phone forever with Brigadier Jaslok's wife.
She is new here, and we were just chatting, and I couldn't be rude. We can go now."
"There's tea Ma," said her younger son, triumphantly, *"I made it."*
She smiled.

"I should've made cha," said her daughter-in-law, *"I am so sorry I am so sick."*
"You're not sick! You are the brightest light in the family, you are a mother,
you are the only person in the family who is doing something about the next generation," declared her devar as he snuck a look at his older brother.
Rani Sahiba laughed so hard her teacup clattered dangerously on the saucer in her bejeweled hand.
"Ashima, never forget, you are a mother, you are a bringer of life," she said to her daughter-in-law.
The Zamindar looked reasonably chastised, a tiny bit remorseful, and plenty aggrandized.
A baby on the way is a joy already.

A few weeks went by and the newborn arrived with a loud healthy cry that gladdened the hearts of all who heard him.
The palace, without the pitter-patter of little feet, had grown too serious in its demeanor, decorum, and decor, a lot of people thought, especially Rani Sahiba.
Now that was about to change.
She held her little grandson and cooed sweet nothings in his ear, as did his father, and his mother, as they passed their little bundle of joy around for introductions.
His kaku was away, and when he returned in a week, he ran to the nursery to say hello to his nephew.
"Look at you!" he said, *"You got your grandfather's nose, your mother's eyes, and my mother's eyebrows. You're so funny, I*
can look at just you and see my whole family in your one little face. You are a family album. Here, go back to your mumma,
she misses you already. I hope someday I have kids half as cute as you."

Boudi smiled as she understood why her devar saw so much in her.
"He sees the world in everybody. It's a certain kind of human being who sees the best and the most expansive version of
another. They don't ridicule or minimize or restrict another, they see them in their every avatar, and they see them with eyes
filled with love. No wonder he saw in me a mother, a writer, a bright light, a whale, a someone who throws up behind hedges,
and none of that was incongruent to him. He valued my feminine fragility and my intellect. And then there are those who can
see nothing good in anybody. All they see are slaves and masters."

And there began her search within herself for herself,
a quest for the inner being that the sages had named Prakriti, Saraswati, Lakshmi,
to name a few, this inner being, the Ashima beyond the Ashima everybody saw and some loved tenderly, as did her mother, her Dida, her nanny, her brother, and her puppy, the Ashima that either blossomed or withered, nay, lived or died amongst microtransactions.

xiii. Digital Art by Walid Sayed (Sayed ©)

12 Fault Lines in the Kingdom of Oedipus Rex

I'm swept up by the romance of this misty morning,
a foggy morning made more mysterious
by bird calls coy and sweet and soft.
My immediate world is perfumed with autumnal scents
suspended in the luminescent morning air.

I look at the tree by my window.
Leaves yellow, orange, and red
glisten on boughs like enchanted ornaments.

The crooked path beckons
out of the backyard through the woods into the glade.
The familiar trail is lost in the haze
a little past the iron gate
right where the brown rabbit has his burrow.

All I can see in the moment is light and fog.
My jacket feels too warm for the day, but it keeps the damp out.
I'm walking to clear my head.
The fog within is poetically mimicking the fog without.
I smirk at my own little observation.

I'm tired now of trying to find my way through the thicket and brush
in this relentless fog,
robbed of the familiar signposts of the persimmon tree,
the brick chimney that tells of a cottage that once stood
on this lovely land, ruins from an idyllic past,
conjuring up visions of simpler sweeter times,
and the lone majestic maple that is gorgeous this time of year.

Everything around me seems unsure and gray and blurry in the fog.
I am walking to clear my head.
The sun's coming up and the fog is thinning slightly.

Now past the clearing I see a clump of elms I've never seen before.
I've never been this far from home into the woods,
but it seems safe enough to be here, so I sit down to rest.

The fog is still warm, and wet, and sweet.
The romance of it all is slightly worn,
but it is still beautiful enough to appreciate.

I look up at the dew-laden boughs of the elms
and touch the bark rough and wet.
Insulated by the fog all I see and all I feel
is curiously magnified and utterly sensuous.
My mind sees this as a visual pun,
"Desire Under The Elms,"
remembering O'Neil and the Greeks,
remembering too how I puked when I first read it all,
ruing the killing, the incest, the insanity,
the betrayal of evolution of billions of years by a foolish boy,
who in the manner of certain usurping princes killed the patriarch,
and claimed his harem.
I understand now its place in the evolution of the individual
and am unfazed by its goriness.

Sunshine has begun to peep above the tops of the trees,
the fog is clearing nicely as I retrace my steps.

I see the woods, the trees, the chimney, differently now.
I have no choice but to make peace with the fact
that there always has been the darker side of life
aided by the soulless among us,
making tragedies of every human tale,
making dead dupes of the simple ones,
nobles of the crafty ones.
Those facts of life are no longer tolerable to me.

This lover of light has relinquished her ego
and accepted her handicap.
Lovers of light are blinded by the light,
just as they would be blinded by the night,
and rendered useless as babes in the woods,
until they learn to see in the dark,
and in the darkness of now,
and of yesterdays, and tomorrows.
This walk through the fog has been good practice for dueling in the dark.

13 Where's Electra?

Has anyone seen Electra?
My friends and I have been looking for her all over the neighborhood.
Is she hiding?
Repressed?
Confused?
Sad?
Shamed?
Indulging in delectable delights away from prying eyes?
Is she bereft and mourning and fighting off suitors Penelope-like?
Is she cold and vain or sweet and maternal?
We found several Oedipii each on an odyssey of his own whilst looking for her.
Is she okay?
Was her Daddy cruel or kind?
And Mommy?
Is she lost?
Where is she?
If you see her, will you tell her we've been looking for her?
Tell her to come out and play in the fresh air and sunshine.

14 Koi Pond

You touch me,
I quiver,
ripples carrying shooting stars.
Beneath the translucent veil,
thoughts red and black
dart about
hoping to come to a fruitful conclusion.
A floating lily catching sunbeams
fills to the brim.
Light spills over.
A drop of hopefulness touches the surface.
A buddha is born.

15 FALL HAIKU

FOLIAGE
swatches sailing down
russet, yellow, mauve, brown, beige
canopy now rug

HARVEST
exotic fruitage
please tease appease the senses
recall Eve's apple

VITAL SIGNS
brittle chill thrills with
the first frost of the year and
I know I'm alive

AUTUMN SKIES
geese, butterflies, larks
make it look so easy,
I could fly to you

BREAKING DAWN
diaphanous mist
conceals you and me this dawn
as light within light

16 The Awful Simplicity of Ten

ONE

a single petal
rose red velvet scent supine
snow white pillowcase

TWO

carmine awakened
surprised by the wind
warmly gathered up in musk

THREE

venturesome brightness
pearl and obsidian eyes
peals of laughter twinkling

FOUR

sugar rush times two
rush, slow down, run, mosey, sleep
dream and learn together

FIVE

copy, model, rebel
coalesce, disperse, return
to love and home

SIX

roots adventitious
and tap recall recursive
journey seed to seed

SEVEN

generations weave
a quilt of traditions real
unreal bittersweet

EIGHT

life ebbs, flows, begins
ends, endlessly organic
builds tribes and nations

NINE

nine lives of each act
of random kindness also
of evil design

TEN

river wends its way
through destiny doership
drenched in rose and musk

When We Were Very Young

"Children have souls that can know without knowing..."
(An Alphaby for my Beautiful Dreamer)

1 An Alphaby for My Beautiful Dreamer

Ask me why I tell you this tale.
Because you need to know my little one,
Children have souls that can know without knowing.
Dear ♫ *baby mine*♫, I love you too much or just
Enough, to tell you what you must not
Forget for as long as you need to remember.
Get the shield of Hercules.
Hire Cinderella's coach.
Instant message Peter Pan to get here quick,
Junior's ready for a bedtime story.
Know this my love that
Love conquers all,
Mastodons, witches, pirates, and all.
Never fear when Spiderman is here.
Only believe.
Perhaps I should tell you
Quixote won.
Ready.
Steady.
Tonight.
Under the
Veil of night,
We will dispel the myth
'Xactly at the stroke of twelve that
Your dreams are locked in
ZZZZZs and are after all just dreams.

2 Colorlines in the Sandbox

My baby loves to sing.
It's nursery rhymes, pop, tv jingles,
all day.

She has a playdate with her classmate,
and I am watching the kids.

She breaks into a Beyonce song
that is on the radio all day these days.
All the kids are singing it,
except her little friend.
"Don't sing that song, my friend,"
she admonishes, *"We don't sing that song."*

"Whyyyy," my baby whines,
stung by her best friend's disapproval.

"Because it's not our culture,"
says her little classmate.

My baby stands in the sandbox,
blinking in confusion and disbelief.
She's never heard this line of logic against her singing.
It's usually, *"Be quiet, I'm trying to concentrate,"*
from a sibling or parent,
or *"Focus on your work"*
to which she always says,
"I do so much better with music."

Her little friend is not having the stony face and the blinking.
She takes tiny deliberate steps toward my baby,
a cute little accusatory finger pointed in her direction,
*"I know your deepest darkest secret.
You are an Oprah watcher."*

Bam! I know this is a reenactment,
and I am sad.

I know this sweet friendship is doomed.
You can't tell friends what songs they can't sing
unless you are willing to lose them.
And lose them you will,
if not the first time, by the fifth time,
you will.

3 The Two Ends of a Telescope

A little boy six or so,
playing soldier out in the backyard,
builds his fortress with young green branches
arching down from an overgrown bush
and a cotton dhurrie he borrowed
from the kitchen floor.

He marshals his troops to victories
around the carrot patch,
the rose bushes,
the plum trees,
and settles down in the shade
with a cup of the bluest Gatorade.

He grows up and goes to war.
His talents as a leader among men
and his courage and forethought
earn him a place among
the best of the best.

He surveys his accomplishments
and wants just one more little thing:
the simplicity of that existence
where one carried no train
behind him,
no worry
before him,
because ♫ the little child inside the man ♫ lives.

xiv. Painting by Pramod Kurlekar (Kurlekar©)

4 Paper Boats on River Time

The moon was big and yellow and cheesy but beautiful
over the silhouettes of pines rustling in the breeze.

Supper had begun at four with carrot soup and croutons,
and had meandered into a tub of mashed potatoes and the tryptophan,
flanked by chicken biryani and banana cream pie.

At seven we wiped the whipped cream off our lips on our sleeves,
our lucky selves drunk on the camaraderie of family and friends.
We'd watched The Oz on the VCR already,
we weren't about to watch it again on TV.
We sneaked off instead onto the deck
to get some fresh air, we said, my cousin and I,
and out there the night was young and carefree.

We were seven and nine, or eight if you insisted upon equality,
for you see, I was seven, my cousin was nine,
and if anybody asked how old "we" were, we simply said "eight."
We shared everything equally.
If we chanced upon a stash of fifteen jellybeans
we took seven each and bit the eighth into halves.
If we had twenty-seven marbles between us
we threw away the "fourteenth."
But I digress.

We were suffering that day from a bad case of cabin fever,
as it had rained five days in a row.
The hurricane had swallowed up half the holiday week
but it had left us with a gushing creek at the edge of the yard,
two or maybe even three feet across,
a mini-Mississippi to my little Colossus.
And as all flowing waters over the centuries
have inspired humankind to build vessels,
ours inspired us to build boats for to carry forth our dreams.

This one sent us hurtling back into the house for a sheaf of papers
with which to build paper boats to float on the stream slick with moonlight.
"Be careful," said my older cousin, ever watchful of the younger me.
I think now that it matters so much that we remain careful in everything we do.
I can hardly believe we pay homage to those ships that came over vast waterways

bearing guns, germs, and steel, and the will to kill the innocent with them all.
We shouldn't reduce the horror to the annual worshipping of the Black Friday.
How should we honor those who suffer still from the wounds of yesterday?

xv. Painting By Pramod Kurlekar (Kurlekar©)

5 Happy Pidgin

I walk into the staffroom to pick up papers to organize.
It's four o'clock.
I just picked up my "three and eleven twelfths" year-old precocious brat,
who insisted on dragging her backpack behind her, loaded with drive-thru toys
to amuse herself, while I "do my stuff" and she's "getting bored waiting to go home."

Everybody loves a baby so she's okay.
Amy said hi and asked me if she could offer her candy.
My baby said yes, I said no, not today, and got two mean looks.

Swati got microbraids she adores, and her husband loathes them.
My baby gushed, *"Ooooo, put beads in them. They'll look even prettier."*
I nodded my assent. I love color and embellishment and juxtaposition
and the fact we're each entitled to simple pleasures.
Swati said she's teaching Proust so she's brushing up on her French.

ESPN's showing a Scripp's Spelling Bee rerun.
A kid can't spell 'howdah' and it's funny to all of us watching,
but the poor kid doesn't get the humor in the situation at all.
He's indignant and unhappy.

Doug asked me if I'd read Yann Martel's *'Life of Pi.'*
I said I would soon, after I'm done with this Jackie Collins.
He asked if I'd ever been to the zoo in Pondicherry.
I know I gave him a look like he'd asked
if I had soaked my head in boiling water.
My bad.
but it takes too long to explain so I said nothing at all.
He'll think I must be perimenopausal,
like my son said, and that's quite alright with me.

Dr. Schweitzer's potted Hanukkah bush sits in the corner
next to his collection of succulents and pothos,
and that reminds me to ask for his recipe for spaghetti with meat sauce.
It's the best in the world!
But he's gone to Cape Cod for his daughter's wedding.
The father of the bride won't be back for a few days,
so I'll water the plants.

Jason who takes care of multimedia, Red Bull,
and the melancholia quotient around here
is a web-surfing late Gen Y blogging whiz kid.
He is savvy beyond belief.
He tunes into what my baby is doing, sorting her toys into two categories:
the ones she likes and the ones she doesn't like,
and makes me feel like a bad mother for not knowing what she likes and what she doesn't like.
No wonder my kids say at least once a day, *"Mom, you don't know anything."*
He found me the cheapest online SAT prep tutor for my oldest.
"Where?" a fellow parent might ask so I found out,
Tuticorin, near Pondicherry, if Doug would care to know.
But Doug's twins are only two so he needn't know.
He plays video games a lot and I really, really, really envy him for it,
for he'll have that in common with his boys.
I wish I knew my way around an Xbox.
My kids might love me a little more if I did but I'm afraid of the backlash I'll generate
when I say among fellow parents that video games and PCs
might be a good thing after all.
They'll never see my reasoning and the proof.

My baby's showing off.
She's taught herself to read with a little help from her brother in first grade.
He's teaching her fractions now, and has told her that her real age isn't three,
but three and eleven twelfths.
"Made in China," I hear her say, as I look for a red pen that seems to have disappeared.
I hear her say that over and over and over.
Maybe my baby can't read all that well yet, and then I see the reason why.
She's reading labels on all her toys like I read labels on food products
which remind me every day I'm feeding my family
too many trans fats and too much sodium and so on,
but that's what they love to eat.
Does that make me a good mother or a bad mother?
Before I can answer that question, she asks me another,
"Mama, were you made in China too?"
It gets a few guffaws and giggles.
My baby is pleased with her joke, and so am I.
I've taught my children to pause for a moment once each day and ask,
"Who am I and what am I doing here?"
I ask myself the same.
I find out I am a visiting parent volunteer trying to help with a school project.
I haven't found that red pen yet and it's getting late.
We're heading home.

xvi. Photograph by Shri J. P. Singh

6 Fairytalia

When I was five, my Nani asked me to read to her.
Much discomfited, I told her I couldn't read the book in my hands,
I was just admiring the pictures.
She asked me if I knew the story of Brer Rabbit.
I didn't.
She asked me if I knew of the four musicians of Bremen.
Nope, never heard of them.
She sighed, I think she was disappointed.
Family folklore says she taught herself to read at three.

This was at Christmas, when we were visiting her.
A few weeks later, a large box arrived in the mail.
In it were two books by Enid Blyton, "The Brer Rabbit Book" and "Brer Rabbit Again."
There was a National Geographic encyclopedia with pictures of people and places I had never seen before.
And the pièce de resistance, the most gloriously bound book,
was a red, white, and gold book with gold on the edges of the pages,
"The World 's Best Fairytales".
In it my Nani had signed her name
with lots of love and kisses,
and given me the book for my birthday.
The illustrations had my head spinning.

My parents read to me every single day.
I wouldn't take no for an answer.
Brer Rabbit was my father's favorite.
My mother read me fairytales.
I laughed, and cried, and rolled with laughter in my new world of make-believe.
I dictated synopses of the stories when my mother wrote to my Nani each week.
Nani would respond to all my messages, and that was such a thrill.
She knew all the "people" I was talking about-
the town mouse, the country mouse, the little match girl, even Rumpelstiltskin.

One evening I had the worst shock of my little life.
My dad was too busy to read to me and my mom said she was too,
and that I should read for myself.
That hurt.
I tried to focus on the letters on the page through my self-righteous tears.
I knew that the tailors were lying to the king.
I also knew that the little boy would laugh at him.
So, I fake-read the story to myself and went to sleep thinking,

"My Nani would never do this to me. She loves the fairytales like I do,
and she truly loves me."
And I went to sleep.

My parents had probably planned the whole thing in advance.
They were *"too busy to read"* again the next evening.
I fought through my tears and fake-read a fairytale again.

That was the sad, sad beginning of the family ailment manifesting itself in me.
I had developed a bad case of Fairytalia.

My parents, in the meantime, were having a relapse of Fairytalia.
One day, my father had to go to the city for work.
He came home with an armful of *Superman* comic books and a Meccano set.
My mother was most indignant
he hadn't told her he was going to the bookstore.
She had wanted a copy of *Rikki Tikki Tavi* and *The Adventures of Winnie the Pooh*.

When she was ten she used to have a pet mongoose she had named Rikki Tikki Tavi.
Pooh Bear was her favorite childhood memory.

Fairytalia has been dutifully passed on to the offspring,
except it's more Nickelodeon and PBS than H.C.Anderson now.
I suppose the ailment mutates over time.

My babies have read every single book about Spot the dog, and Arthur and friends.
I suppose my Nani would be happy to know somebody in this new generation
taught himself to read at three, just like she had.

xvii. Photograph by Sonali Deuskar Gurpur

7 Hot Mix

It's tea time in Mumbai,
a *glucotse biscut ani chaha* affair, mainly.

The grownups opt for the biscuits.
They're easier to store on a saucer.

My cousin and I reach for the messier Hot Mix,
charmuri, sev, moth, and hot stuff.

My little cousin might have been bored,
or OCD, or just bored and 7 years old.

On a white paper napkin,
he had the ingredients lined up,

the white churmuri, the brown moth,
the golden sev, in separate piles.

He scooped them up
one at a time and ate them.

I asked him if he liked them better that way.
"Yes and No," he said.

"Ah!" I thought,
"I have never heard that one before."

I was shook that my baby cousin
had just introduced me to a mind-blowing concept

that had compounded the complexity
of my world exponentially.

8 Stranger Danger

There's one bit of life advice my father gave me
that I thought was merely a piece of scientific trivia.
I was looking in the mirror and fixing the parting of my hair.
He said, *"You don't look exactly like your image, you know that?*
The lateral inversion changes your face,
the light falls on you from different angles,
the colors you wear affect your image.
You have no idea how different you are from the image you see right now.
I can see that. You too need to remember that."

Light, refraction, parallax, reflection, optical illusions,
the many versions of change blindness,
all had held an immense fascination for me as external events.
Little did I realize all of that happens on the inside too.

Seeing clearly truly is an inside job.

xviii. Painting by Sukumar Deuskar (Deuskar ©)

9 Here and Now

This moment falls from my hands like a broken string of pearls.
Nanoseconds scattering on the floor of cold unheeding barren gray stone.
Time evanescent evaporates instantaneously.

A moment hurls itself out the window faster than the speed of light,
a wave that made its humble way from the lapping waves of the waters of yesterday.

Grandma used to say there used to be an incandescent streetlamp where there is now a tube light.
She fondly remembered the days of yore when a lamplighter used to shimmy up a ladder each new evening
to trim the wick and set it aflame as the family gathered around the radio for the nightly news broadcast.

This very moment a son is born to the salt merchant's son's son's son.
Five generations have lived on our street and have each sported the same bulbous nose.
Nothing changes, yet everything is different every day.

10 Homesick

This is a love letter to the Kashmir of my memories. Many years ago, I saw this carved in stone in Srinagar - "Gar firdaus bar-rue zamin ast, hami asto, hamin asto, hamin ast." ("If there is a heaven on earth, it's here, it's here, it's here." - Amir Khusrau.)

8 O'clock
"The hot water is ready," Mummy said.
I unlidded my sleepy eyes,
adjusting to the slanting light coming through the blinds.
I slowly woke up to the whitewashed room,
colonial in proportions, pre-independence in décor.
I took in a deep breath of fresh mountain air
still unfamiliar to my Hyderabadi lungs.
This felt like my new home, oddly.
I lollygagged, idling gloriously in the feeling
of the official first morning of a summer holiday.
The hot water would be just fine a few degrees cooler.

It was my parents' seventeenth wedding anniversary.
We were in Srinagar, the three of us, and my grandma, on vacation,
more than a thousand miles away from home.

We'd arrived just eight hours ago to a crisp midsummer night in the valley
and been ushered into the sitting room of this lovely guest house.
A warm cup of wonderfully fragrant tea was thrust into my hands.
I was enraptured by the affectionate friendliness of the two people we'd met so far,
the one serving chai in a beautiful green *firan,*
and the one who had chauffeured us to the *dak* bungalow.
It certainly didn't feel like canned tinny affected touristy affection.
These people were the salt of the earth.

On the way to the guest house, there were The Boulevard, the glistening Dahl dotted with houseboats, the *Char Chinar*, now three, explained the chauffeur, as one had died.

… Have you ever seen a houseboat by night, gondola-like, bobbing on the dark water, a light behind the curtain in a window, lights reflected below multiplying light? …
Oh, you should!

xix. Painting by Dina Nath Walli (Walli ©, A house boat in moonlight, 1967)

People were walking around at midnight, tourists and locals alike.

Little shanty shops selling *waazwaan*, carved mementos, silken and woolen wear lined the streets.

"This is a party that should never end," thought my sixteen-year-old self.

It was like my mother's instinctual ear picked up on that thought.

She asked the chauffeur if it was safe to be out walking this late.

He said yes, and that summers are short here,

and that he would love to park by the side of the pavement

so we could look around, and not a fly would hurt us.

Or, perhaps, we would like to return another night

if we were too tired from our bus ride here from Jammu.

Srinagar seemed like the friendliest place on earth.

11 Call of the Valley

The valley in the summertime had been beautiful.
I couldn't believe I would be traveling to Srinagar again.
This time, in the wintertime.
I could not wait to get there.
The flight from New Delhi to Srinagar
took us from the bustle of a megalopolis
to the calm of a quiet gem of a mid-sized city.

xx. Painting by Dina Nath Walli (Walli ©, Village Bemuna Kashmir, 1961)

Much was different.
Much had changed in the six years
since our last trip to Kashmir.
We were still in mourning.
My sweet mother had passed away.

The shock was just wearing off.
The reality of loss was setting in.
Two years had passed.
It still felt odd to wake up in the morning and not see her.
Except now it took only three seconds to adjust to that fact,
instead of half the morning.

As the wheels touched down on the tarmac
a new never-before-seen gut-wrenching sadness hit hard.
"This trip to Srinagar is going to be very different from the last one,"
I thought to myself.
I just hadn't known how prophetic that feeling was.

At first, the only difference one noticed on the drive through the city
was that everybody was bundled up, some carrying *kangris*,
little clay vessels containing burning coal,
a traditional portable heater.
Almost right after that one perceived a deep sadness on each face
that passed by the window.

xxi. Painting by Dina Nath Walli (Walli ©, Chinars in Autumn, 1941)

We'd watched news reports on TV about tensions in the city
but you never really know what's happening someplace until
you see it in person.
And there it was, a public transportation bus with a gaping hole in it.
The chauffeur pointed to it and said, *"That is the new Kashmir."*
His face betrayed no emotion, oddly.
I think he had been sad before he saw the blown-up bus,
and he couldn't feel any more sadness than he did already.
Like us, he appeared to be in mourning,
and had transitioned from shock to acceptance,
just like we had, over the years.
He said," *For a month, the extremists blew up one vehicle a day.*
People were afraid to travel, fearful of leaving home.
Schools suffered, work suffered.
Everything is still a mess.
We don't know how long this spell of calm will last."

"But why? Why is this happening?" we asked.
He said plenty and we understood little.
It's difficult to know what's happening to the local population
when you are an outsider, typically ensconced in a safe society.
You don't know how terror works, and might never truly understand.

Our chauffeur and guide appeared to imply
that terrorism is the only religion of the terrorist,
that it was showmanship,
that it was unspeakable crimes in broad daylight,
that it was impersonal to a fault,
that the cruelty was the point…

xxii. Painting by Dina Nath Walli (Walli ©, Mar canal, 1946)

Never preach to those being attacked by terrorists,
unless you have successfully undone terrorism
and its aftermath.
You'll just look clueless or heartless.

It was a bizarre vacation.
There was beauty.
There was deep mourning.
There was fresh evidence each new day
of the nightmare that was on its way,
and it appeared that nothing was making sense to anybody
but the terrorist.

We went to Dachigam with friends
and saw new sights and old.
Everything looked different this time around,
with the poplars clothed in gold
and the chinars in russet,
festive and elegant.

When beauty and sadness are inextricably mixed
 you mostly notice the sadness,
especially if you are sad already.

On our last day in the city
we went out to lunch with the family we'd traveled with.

As we sat down at our table,
the owner of the restaurant walked up to us
and said we needed to finish lunch in thirty minutes,
and exit the building.
"The two gentlemen seated at the table next to us said so," he added,
in a manner so unhurried and affable,
we assumed his serious face was a natural expression
of his unique personality.
He was nice, just reserved, we surmised,
and completely missed his import.

We turned to look at the two gentlemen
seated at the table next to us.

They looked glum, reading a pamphlet each.
Neither spoke nor made eye contact.
They weren't eating.
They looked like locals and were dressed in jeans and sweaters.
Tall, slender, modern, with longish beards and sideburns,
they were a little scruffy but appeared to be educated.

We were clueless.
We most certainly did not pick up on the extreme gloominess
of those around us.

When *waazwaan* and sadness are inextricably mixed
and you are very, very hungry,
your appetite whetted by walking in the crisp mountain air,
all you see is *waazwaan.*

Our brains manufactured the normalcy that was so clearly missing in the room.
Our brains completely overrode the peculiarity of the request
from fellow diners that we rush our meal and leave.
Who says that, and why?!
We are primarily social animals

who instinctively trust those we share personal space with.
And that's how malefic forces enter our personal spaces.

We feasted on the best *rogan josh* and *gushtaba* that afternoon.
We took our own sweet time.
Not once did the owner remind us of the time,
nor did our neighbors at the next table.

We dipped our oily fingers in warm bowls of lemon water,
wiped them off on crisp serviettes,
and piled into the car to go back to the hotel.

A half-hour later our chauffeur came by to tell us
that the white Ambassador that had been parked next to us
outside the restaurant,
blew up ten minutes after we had driven off.

Yes, that was our introduction to terrorism.
It creeps into societies, into our homes, and schools and businesses,
gently, discreetly, looking very legit in form and function.

The oddness is almost within normal range.
Throw in a well-thought-out alibi, and the oddness turns into ordinariness,
and almost nobody knows how to handle it.

I pray there is hope yet for Kashmir and its wonderful, friendly, resilient people.
Let's give them a voice, a thriving economy, and freedom from terror.

I Went to the Animal Fair

"…I WANT, declared the elephant in the room …

1 Splat!

Bug on the windshield of Life, am I,
irregular blot,
still wet and gooey,
contemplating the landscape whizzing by,
taxing what little is left of my mind.

2 Going Somewhere?

Rodent treadmill on warp speed,
fur flying,
feet slipping,
heart pounding meaninglessly.

Is there anything sorrier
than my little gerbil
on his little plastic train to nowhere?

3 Furball

I got two puppies last summer,
and on a whim named them
Desire and Disappointment.
Now I am stuck with them both.
They confuse me when they're together,
jostling and at one another's throats.
One won't leave the other alone.
They're sucking up my oxygen.

They're no longer novel.
Desire doesn't age very well.
Disappointment, on the other hand,
is easier on the eye as time goes by,
but is not what I want.
I tried to give them away
like sick puppies,
but went back for them anyway.

"Give one away and let each
have a home to himself.
They don't get along very well,
you know that," suggested a friend.

"Which one?" I asked, a little too quickly.

"You would be the best judge of that,"
said my PC friend.

"How about both?" I asked facetiously.

Here I am several weeks later,
with both Desire and Disappointment
asleep at my feet,
having just been fed on my peace of mind.
I'll let the sleeping dogs lie.
I'll worry another day
about what precisely
to do with them.

4 It's Not Much of a Life Without You

Daisies are the friendliest flowers, but I didn't plant any this year.
Instead, I lavished time, space, manure, on gorgeous little sunflower stand-ins,
black-eyed Susans, beautiful in their own right.

And here's my puppy, all of six months, being bad.
She's dug up the flower bed, harried the cat, chewed up my flip-flops.

I get her fancy new collar off, put her in the sink, wash the mud off,
deal with the wet dog stink.
The mirror's fogged up, the sink's clogged.

But that mess has to wait.
"I HATE cleaning.
I could've thrown the baby out with the bathwater, you know,"
I say to my trusting pooch.
She wags her tail.

She's cut through the crap. She knows I'm nothing without her.
Words mean nothing to one who knows the language of the heart.
She's all fluffed and dried, asleep on the carpet.

I do what mamas do, hold my breath, and clean the sink.
I feel like a lot of negativity left with that dirty water.
The mirror's not foggy anymore.

4 It's Not Much of a Life Without You

5 "I Want!" Declared the Elephant in the Room

I was wandering through
my brand-new home
and did a double-take.

Adjacent to the doorway,
leading out of the hallway
was another door,
one I'd never seen before
or perhaps hadn't noticed.

On the door was a silver-grey banner
with a little elephant in black outline
that had a pink petunia on its head.

Behind him in a procession
were lined up the letters:
"I WANT "
in a nice large font.

I reached for the doorknob
and mindlessly turned it clockwise.

Then it started:
A trickle at first,
a trinket or two,
a big box of chocolates
from the chocolatier new,
a stuffed baby giraffe
in a tux so handsome,
a rug for my room
that cost a king's ransom,
a boom box that boomed
too loud to bear,
the kiss for Snow White
that dislodged the pear,
a porcelain dove
with beautiful eyes,
a stork, a bear
a harmonica that flies,

the leaky faucet
from Lacrimose Co.,
now with a nice fat stopper
to end its woe,
luggage that looked like
it'd been around the world,
an exquisite desk
of rosewood burled.

Suddenly,
I stood
in a room
chock-full
with answered prayers.

6 Zebra Crossing

Why did the chicken cross the road?
Because he's chicken, he was running away from a problem.

Cluck cluck, shuffle shuffle, cluck cluck, shuffle shuffle,
on the black and white striped path.

A truth and a lie, a truth and a lie…
he didn't know the lights were about to change.

He felt the zing of a plucked tail feather.
Screech! Squawk Squawk! Squawk!

He turned around.
His problem had caught up with him.

7 Swamp ʻer Wimp

Every dog needs a trainer,
that is an established fact.
Or he'll never be housebroken or free of fleas.
He'll pee on every rug he meets,
he'll eat off the dinner table,
he'll chew up the children's books and shoes.
You know, he'll be a problem puppy,
and there'll be folks who'll want to put him to sleep.

Enter: The Dog Whisperer

She said to me,
"We have a problem on our hands.
The boys have tied a can on a string to the
scrawny neck of the mutt,
and he is a biter full of mange.
My staff will not touch him.
They want the dog catcher to euthanize him.
I'm not sure that's the only way out.
His file name's Wimp.
It was Swamp,
I changed it to Wimp.
We'll see what we can do.
I had him moved to another shelter.
They can fumigate him, and wash him,
and teach him to sit.
That'll be a good beginning.
They are a no-kill shelter,
but even they have their limitations.
He bites, he's gone."

8 Protect Your Fur Babies

I just checked -
the cat's NOT in his cradle.
I set his water out for him on the patio.
There was a copycat moon waving at me from the water bowl.

I looked up,
and there was the harvest moon,
full-bellied, birthmarks and all,
swinging low, rotund, and shiny, like Cinderella's chariot.

I looked again at the copycat moon.
Our cat is black,
all black, not a sock, not a single spot,
unblemished unlike the moon.

I inhaled the cold autumnal aromatic mix
of decaying leaves and air purged of its summer scents.
The innards of the jack-o'-lantern remained on the compost heap,
orange in their shallow grave, the seeds rotting yellow teeth.

The witching hour is near.
I must find KitKat.
He's more panther now though,
a high-wire act.

9 Pussy Cat

It's June.
The monsoon has dumped half a river on the jungle.
Rivulets trickle prettily down mossy embankments.
The canopy is rich with fresh foliage.
The vines are taut and plump with sap.
The forest floor is damp and slightly cool in the morning air.
The sickly-sweet stench of burgeoning summer fruit hangs in the air.
The seeming stillness of the forest is punctuated by the flight of flies,
the squawking of parrots, and the rustle of creatures of the night
coming home to roost.

High above on a wide strong branch, I spy a black panther with her eyes shut.
Not a twitch, not a sound, and not quite camouflaged in her emerald halo,
she's a coiled bolt of black lightning, a bowstring at rest ready to snap
at the lightest touch of an arrow and archer.
I imagine her eyes of cold yellow fire burning brightly in her face like night,
hypnotizing in the constancy of a gaze I wouldn't dare to meet,
the sheathed fangs and claws, the pink tongue, the jaws of doom.
This is not your average house cat, though she looks like one.
Mine barely ever catches a mouse, this one's devoured bison and buck.
I wouldn't say, *"Here, kitty, kitty"* even under my breath around here.
My place is at my desk by my window, my kitty sitting by my side,
as I sip coffee and take in the news.

Ekphrasis

muse of my muse …

1 ♫ **The Dark Side of the Moon** ♫

I am driving west ♫ on a dark desert highway. ♫
In my rearview mirror, I catch a fleeting reflection
of a single point of light atop the ribbon of a road,
a gorgeous rising full moon just above the horizon.
I flip a coin to decide if I'll take this exit or the next.
My eyes are tired, ♫ my soul so weary. ♫
I find a motel, flip the lights out,
and rest my cheek on ♫ the flip side of the pillow. ♫
The air conditioner hums a lullaby.
The desert has consumed me.

Somewhere out there on the flip side of the moon
lies a still, dark, sea of tranquility, a desert like this one.
Perhaps a weary soul sleeps there too,
a moon cricket outside his window, his alarm clock set to 6 a.m.,
when my moon and his cease to exist.

2 Starry Night

Labyrinth in the sky,
needlepoint of Light and Darkness,
each showing off her more photogenic side.

I walk through the maze
a ♫ Lucy in the sky with diamonds. ♫
Music plays softly
just out of reach,
drawing me deeper and deeper into the maze.

I work my way out of the maze,
and a big yellow moon is my only witness.
I made it!
I made it out of the dark night of the soul,
and nobody knows.
The village is asleep,
the lights are dim,
I'll sleep too,
and the sun shall greet me tomorrow
like nothing ever happened.

We'll get coffee and go about our day,
griping and moaning and counting our lucky stars,
as usual.

Every night now
I'll look out the window,
I'll wink at the moon.
She knows.

3 Mona Lisa Smile

Smile Mona Lisa!
You're on camera.
You're the subject,
the object,
of microscopic study.

Your eyes, your lips,
your unspoken words,
are inkblots to us.
Can't see you whole,
plain, and human.

4 Manipulating Mona

"There's something about Mona."
"She's a fox."
"She's a stupid cow."
"An old tart."
"She's of royal lineage,
"She's smiling at the beholder."
"Nah, she's tolerating the beholder."

"She's tired."
"She's elated."
"She's celebrating the birth of her third baby."
"She's nuts."
"She's a savant."
"She speaks in riddles like the Sphinx."
"She's dead fish on ice."
"She's Mt. Fuji capped with ice."
"A pickaxe wouldn't hurt her, would it?"

"Lisa Gherardini Giocondo?
It's really Leo in drag."
"No, she's his chick."
"She's only famous for having been in Napoleon's bedroom."
"She's overrated."
"She's underrated."
"She belongs to France."
"No to Italy."
"She looks on the world with love anyhow."

5 Almost David

Please pardon the seeming arrogance,
it is really a hard-won sense of self.
It wasn't easy to be hacked away at,
gouged, chipped, broken, analyzed,
critiqued, questioned, measured endlessly.

Blockhead,
far from the quarry I came from,
abandoned in the churchyard.
Rain, sleet, wind, time,
ran their greedy fingers over me.
I was told I was given to Michelangelo.

Only now I'm beginning to see
the purpose of that existence.
The toes are ten.
The slingshot's done.
The eyes and nose are coming along.
The air of readiness is already here,
moments away from "The Moment"
that holds a divine spark,
and transforms readiness into
responsible action.

The Evolution of Eve

"... Dance me into the night Underneath the moon shining so bright Turning me into the light ..."
(Dark Waltz by Frank Musker / Matteo Saggese / Umberto Morasca)

1 Roses that Grow by the River Juliet

An offering for those who drank the poison in good faith

The poison I had drunk.
There was no more to say,
except goodbye and be well.

Drunk as a Dodo
you might say I was,
and as extinct.

The bard had immortalized the moment,
and I relived it over and over and over.

The poison I had drunk,
because the Lethe was ice.

Hell had frozen over.
Who cared anymore,
now that neither thorns
nor coals could hurt anymore?

I thank the god of small things
for taking over for me,
for cradling that infant spark of life,
that magic seed,
that could possibly grow
and bloom where planted

into a tree with no name,
a partridge in it
♫ my true love gave to me ♫
on that first day of Lent.

The cycles of life must run their course
in this realm of living and dying.

Fall must follow summer,
resurrection fall,
December in between.
and rivers must flow into oceans.

Deities cruel or kind must be appeased
with offerings that please their capricious appetites.

When all have been served to their satisfaction,
the Trickster whispers,
"Turn around and look,
look at how funny you are,
you, a river, dragging the ocean behind you."

xxiii. Mandala art by Sumita Samant (Samant ©)

2 The Chumpion of Lost Causes

Sharmila is so naïve.
She can't pick between prudence and courage.
She flogs dead horses.
She allows herself to be found traipsing through the tulips.
She's a slow unlearner.
She loves her unteacher.
She wants 364 unbirthdays.
What she resists persists.
She depotentiates herself, silly goose,
until her soul screams," STOP."

xxiv. Vintage Art (IndSk)

3 Sharmila at Home

A house on a busy street,
cold, white, locked, large,
marble floors,
a mirror in the foyer.

The lady of the house peers in the mirror,
sees herself,
a wisp of gray in her hair,
a perfect sari.

The mirror shatters,
she walks away,
stepping on shards of glass
like they might be petals.
Her footprints, a dark *rangoli* in her wake,
mock those who stop and stare and say,
"Oh, what a beautiful home you have."

4 The Last Brick

Sharmila's house was built
brick by boring brick
over the period of a year and a half.
They had painstakingly picked out
the eggshell taupe for the walls,
the oyster shell nightlights,
the crackled porcelain drawer pulls,
the crystal chandeliers.
They upgraded from tile to white marble
when it had almost been too late,
had it not been for an indulgent foreman
who wrote a note to the shop
saying he was not satisfied
with the quality of the supplies
and asked for a refund,
which they honored.

It stood in its grandeur,
a shelter from the elements,
a testament to industry,
and upward mobility,
but it couldn't stand the pressure
from within.
It exploded one day
from the echoes of a silent scream
pent up so long in Sharmila's soul,
it shattered every gleaming window,
the stemware,
every lamp, every light,
every piece of ornately carved furniture,
each beating heart in its ineffectual ribcage,
and every pillar and post
of the once stately manor.

That last brick lies on the ground,
an epitaph to what could have been
a happy home.

5 Shame

Shame on you, you Jezebel you.

Serves you right Lot's wife.

Scheherazade you've been bad.

♫ *Roxanne, you don't care if it's wrong or if it's right*♫

Bathsheba, weren't you married to Uriah the Hittite?

Sara wore pink with red,
and did not even cover her head
when she went to the grocery store.

Sita irked our ire
after she had walked through fire.

'Mary' is your name, you said?
And you are from Magdala, not Nazareth?

Shame on you, you Jezebel you.

6 Negative Image

Before digital photography
you couldn't have a photograph
unless there was a negative first.

The light and shade were reversed,
that which was black was white,
and vice versa.

In the excavation of the authentic Self
comes a point in the inner journey
when the exact same thing happens.

Your roadmap warps,
the road goes topsy-turvy,
you are lost in a land of opposites.

Your best years become your worst,
your worst tormentors your best teachers.
It is all about finding balance

via a newfound vision of things
where nothing is perfect,
and we're all too human, and the better for it.

7 Filigree as a Fact of Life

There is that matter of the unreckonable shock
                    of alternating association and dissociation.
        light then darkness,
          hot after cold,
            love followed by unlove,
              good upon the heels of evil,
                a little truth mixed in with a bunch of lies,
wherein each one pierces through the other,
      offering patterns for our review,
        for the human mind ceaselessly tries to make sense of the seeming nonsense.
             We find ourselves yoking together polarities.
When heat cuts through a metal chimney letting light through,
      a filigreed lantern is born,
         charming one and all with its artistic shadow.
 The little meadow at the park
        tells stories of the neighborhood.
Ropes of trodden paths loop over untrodden terrain.
              The path's mostly sand and gravel.
     Little Johnny was here on his tricycle
           while his mommy walked beside him.
The grass is a mess over here because a dachshund and a corgi got into a fight.

    A bright pink cloud peeps through a canopy of little dark green
leaves,
    the brightness appears brighter,
        the darkness darker.
      A spark of understanding comes alive in the murkiness of unknowing,
    a little light piercing through the darkness,
       and often, one wouldn't exist without the other ...

8 That Topsy Turvy Feeling

Facetious self,
lost in translation between
what is, what was, what ought to be?
Disoriented,
alone,
regrets everything and nothing.
The chirrup of cicadas
inside the cranium
create a harrowing din.

9 Shakuntala

It is always February in the land of those who wait.
Spring is just beyond reach, just as is joy, and is speech.
There is silence cold as ice for the songbirds have fled,
and have not returned yet to the splendor of a spring awakening.

The buds on trees hold promise but no proof that promises are kept.
The winter wheat is still green in the fields.
The foal and fawn haven't yet been born.
The ants have gone missing, the peacock hasn't been seen preening.

The bees are huddled in their hives,
the bears in their caves, the rabbits in their burrows.
The fish and the mermaid have stayed low to stay alive,
as the pond froze in patches in the chill of winter.

The smell of winter is the smell of absence.
It is the taunt of the memory of fragrant limes and jasmine sweet.
It is the cruel longing for the first droplets of rain after summer's heat.
February reeks of the dark, and dank, and the decaying.

10 Struggle

A chrysalis is worn, and wet,
and refuses to dry its wings.

A tigress finds the cage door open,
but is imprisoned by her memories.

A newborn gasps involuntarily,
and thinks his lungs are burning.

A rock skips on water too far
for it has forgotten how to sink.

I waver a few moments too long,
unsure of my self-worth.

11 Ode to a New Song

I gave away love I didn't have,
wiped away tears my eyes couldn't shed,
sent missives with postage a few pennies short,
learned to play poker with just half a deck,
gave gifts of peace I didn't own,
and found the spark I had lost.

That all-disturbing photon of light
melted my defenses
against an unrelenting world,
and I found if you trust you are trusted,
if you love you are loved,
if you hate you are hated.

I broke down walls
and let the world fall in.
I sprouted wings
and learned to sing
a new song.
Come sing with me.

I unraveled the knots within
through long sleepless nights,
laughed hard at jokes never told,
looked at life anew,
and learned to smile again.
Smile back at me.

I slipped free of that last shackle,
winked back at the mysteries of life,
took one long draught of elixir
that keeps the shadows at bay,
and danced the night away.
Come dance with me.

12 PARIS

Yet again burns a funeral pyre,
an end of corpus, and mind, and judgment,
the end of decisions, miracles, and mistakes alike.
Blood dries, wounds hurt no more, and won't ever again.
There, Nostradamus could not have said it better himself.
The daughter of Cebren flung herself into the fire too late to no avail.

13 Dualism and Beyond

Welcome to my humble abode.
These double doors
are enchanted.
If you wish me well,
Say, *"Open Sesame."*
Oops, wrong story.
Say, *"Hello,"*
and stay to visit,
make the world a better place,
charm the goodness
out of all muddle-mixes,
for where there is peace,
and an absence of fear,
an abiding confidence that all is well
resides beyond Dualism.

14 Splash!

Feeling empty as a coelenterate,
primal emptiness,
but for the first time,
without primal fears.

I've been an amoeba,
this is an advancement.
Maybe one day I'll wash ashore,
an oddity with bulging eyes,
a dead giant squid.

Children building castles
in the sand
will write me an epitaph,
"Here lie Squidward's Hopes and Dreams."

Perhaps a stingray I'll be.
Anemones will wilt in my dark shadow.
Clownfish will dart away.

Maybe I'll be that clownfish,
and befriend a mermaid,
and see she does not turn to foam.

Maybe I'll rise from the ocean foam,
a pearl of a woman.

xxv. Photograph by Sonali Deuskar Gurpur

15 Creation Destruction Preservation

Have you ever made an omelet
without breaking eggs?
I tried.
I ate air.

Was ever a forest cleared
so you could build your house
where once lived
deer, and rabbits, and wolves?

Did you ever relinquish
a dream
so another
could take its place?

Did you ever
set a butterfly free
and have it come back
sit on your knee?

16 Star Girl

An homage to some amazing women, who were amazing through everything, at all junctures in their lives, whether being celebrated, or burned at the stake.

We've waited for the first snow of the season
for a while now, especially my little son has, impatiently.
I peek out the picture window
looking for signs of a wintry mix.
The weatherman was dead wrong.
The sky is so beautiful it makes me smile.
Ouch! I need lip balm.
The winter sky is clearer than ever,
Orion strides confidently, Sirius at his heel.

At my feet,
incongruous on a woebegone Sunday night,
blooms a flirty blood-red Amaryllis,
in a pot of blue and white chinoiserie.

♫ *Starry starry night* ♫
I wish I may I wish I might wish upon a star tonight,
or on the geometry of lilies,
mandalas on my freshly mopped floor,
Om Hrim,
Star of David,
Najmat Dawud.

A lily white,
fragrant, pure, and bright,
grows next to the red one,
in her own pot of clay.

Sweet baby Jehanne
Fleur-de-lys,
martyred at scarcely nineteen,
ended a war of a hundred years.
You'll live in our hearts forever.

My eyes are drawn toward the picture frame on the shelf,
compelled by the star shapes of yellow trumpet lilies,
seven on a stalk, proclaiming their brassiness
on a golden afternoon.

I get up to feed the fish,
the sea cucumber, the sea urchin, and the starfish,
but it's only the aforementioned star shape I see with new eyes,
stargazer that I am tonight.

There's something different about him tonight.
Aha! Pentagram not hexagram,
and if he should lose a limb he'll grow another,
like starfish, reflections of celestial stars on the ocean floor
that look so like stars come down from the firmament.

On the refrigerator door is a calendar
with golden pentacles I've given my son
on days he's done his chores,
seals of approval that'll earn him cash,
a work ethic, and some righteous amour-propre, I hope.
Solomon was given both knowledge and wisdom, I'm reminded,
and I wish the same for my cherub.

I look out again.
Okay, so it's getting cloudy now.
I can't see Cetus, nor Andromeda, or Perseus.
It'll snow, or sleet, or rain, we'll see,
and my lilies will wilt with the heater on.
I'll water them well, poor dears,
and let them pretend it's the Sundarbans in here,
and I'll be happy for the ♫ bare necessities, ♫
and Raksha, Baloo, Bagheera.
And Kaa?
The googly-eyed one who hissed ♫ *"Trussssssssst in me"?* ♫
Should I?
Trust?
Him?

Ha! I won the staring contest.

Images of a littoral mangrove flood my imagination,
Edenlike in their beauty.

I have the distinct sensation of shedding exteriors.
A clay mold splits open, and I step out Woman,
red-haired in a blue denim dress,
my baby boy on my hip.

17 Alice Matter, Mad as a Hatter Said,
"All hail the Dark Queen"

Barging down the river a mile,
I once met a crocodile,
whose smile
I didn't really care for.
I asked my maid-in-waiting
if she'd do a little baiting,
and have the ax man
do away with that which I abhor.
Now I beam a benign smile,
it's pure pleasure, there's no guile.
Believe me.
I love my shoes, my clutch, and the beautiful Nile.

18 Winter Fallow

Cold as cold can be, this winter left me free, to be my own person.

What joy it is to birth the Self, and to love your new baby,
the cherubic delight that you are in plain sight,
that you hadn't seen before, in forty years or more, but now you know.

Now you see who you can be when you've given up
on the self-sabotage that once looked a lot like living.

xxvi. Painting by Pramod Kurlekar (Kurlekar ©, 'A classical dancer', 2023)

19 Humsini

Humsini's parents had hoped to have a baby girl
to offset the rambunctiousness of their two boys.
And here she was.

Intelligent observant eyes,
pert little nose,
a very ready smile,
uncommon in newborns.
Her parents named her Humsini,
little swan.

How prescient was that!
Humsini grew up to be
an extraordinarily graceful dancer.

I have watched this child grow up,
and have learned so much from her.
She hates little, fears nothing, and is humble to a fault.

She has all the noble qualities
associated with her namesake
and none of the haughtiness.

The baby girl doesn't just excel at Bharatanatyam,
she's an engineer too,
a good one,
much sought after in the aeronautical industry.

She models Kanjivaram saris on runways all over India.
She says it's a lot easier than dancing,
you get most of the day to yourself,
there's little to practice.
She says she studies eight hours a day when she travels.
She has a model friend whose mom travels with them.
Sabitha Aunty takes care of food, laundry, and sightseeing,
in whichever city they are in.

Yes, of course, she can fly a plane.
She's been doing that since she was seventeen,
that's how she got into aeronautical engineering.
Her brothers took flying lessons,
and so did she.

People are amazed when they find out
she speaks six languages,
Tamil, Tulu, Kannada, Malayalam, Hindi, and English.
She says she has no choice.
Her paternal grandparents live in Kasaragod,
they speak Tamil at home.
Her maternal grandparents live in Mangalore,
they speak Tulu at home.
She grew up in Chennai,
where her parents settled down when she was a baby.
Her best friend growing up was her neighbor from Almora, Uttarkhand.
They watched T.V. sitcoms together every day after school.
That's where she picked up idiomatic Hindi.

One time, jealous me, who speaks only two languages,
asked her. *"If you hold your nose and speak Malayalam,
doesn't it turn into Tamil?"*
She rolled her eyes and said, *"It's so much more than that, Aunty"*,
then she giggled self-consciously at my pathetic ignorance.
I felt very poorly that the true multilingual gene had passed me by.
After all, my mother spoke fluent Hindi, English, and Bengali.
My dad speaks, in addition to that, fluent Telugu and Gorkhali too.
He even reads and writes comfortably in Urdu.
And here's little old me, struggling with French 101,
my feeble attempt at gaining a third language.

This child, now a young woman,
weaves in and out of cultures, and languages, and societies,
with grace beyond compare.
I tell her sometimes she needs to write a curriculum
for the rest of us, to teach us how to do what she does effortlessly.
She laughs, she sparkles,
but I don't think she knows how she does it.

I have thought about her amazing ability to learn so much so well,
and to get along with almost anybody anywhere
so, perhaps, I can craft a curriculum
I can learn from and share with others too.

I don't think it's a "things to do to be like Humsini" list.
It's a "how to think like Humsini" list.
As I said, she hates little, fears nothing, and is humble to a fault.

20 Transmutation

A portal opened.
I fell asleep one person,
and awoke another.
I had walked through the looking glass,
and smashed the hourglass.
all on account
of having vowed myself
brutal honesty.
I won't dare shut my eyes
to this ♫whole new world.♫

21 New Beginnings

Looking out the window has been boring lately.
The trees are bare, the grass is brown,
I'm lucky if I see a bright cardinal or two a week.
I stare at the expanse of brown and gray mindlessly.

If you cut the trunk of that tree across
there'd be a hundred concentric rings,
one light, one dark, one light, one dark,
ripples spreading outward to eternity,
a Big Bang of wood and sap,
raw material that gave a robin a home,
a squirrel food,
a gardener shade,
a breeze dry leaves to toy with.

The bare boughs sprout buds again
this bitterly cold January
in a renewal that defies logic.

Has the sensuous business
of bringing life forth
been going on for months
right outside my window?

22 Persephone's Reprieve

The pomegranate split open,
jeweled on the inside.
The sunlight stopped being wishy-washy
around the whitewashed room,
and turned into liquid love,
pouring itself into me.
Buds arranged themselves in whorls on
dark bark, stark against the winter sky,
to celebrate.

The play of shadow and light
on a weakly warm wintry morning
bleakly lit up an imaginary archway
on the solid wall.
Suddenly I knew
why the caged bird sings.
I sang too,
to my utter disbelief,
to celebrate.

Songs forgotten over a lifetime
came back to me and made perfect sense.
My feet could almost feel
the sweet tickle of grass
growing unabashedly under my feet.
Memories of fireflies in June
put on a show
in the theater of my mind,
to celebrate.

xxvii. Photograph by Sonali Deuskar Gurpur

23 Complimentary Angels

Part I
Lame duck vs. Dumb luck

I Aphrodite,
♫ *beautiful but flighty,* ♫
walking through the forest,
trust me I'm no florist,
head of Hephaestus,
poisonous as asbestos,
on a silver salver,
beautiful disaster,
here dear Athene,
an offering for thee.

Part II

Bookends
Sweet Aphrodite,
I thought you're high and mighty.
Thank you for the present.
It's the perfect accent
among the family heirlooms,
gold, silver, Pegasus, grooms.
And look a matching pair,
no more solitaire,
the gift of Medusas' hair,
Perseus brought me there.

24 Blame It On Her(A)

Tiresias revisited.
Tiresias unbound.
Tiresias interrogated.
Tiresias absolved of all wrongdoing.
Hera's left holding the chopping block.

25 Shadow Play

Devi with the four arms,
why do I love you and fear you
in equal measure?
Who are you?
I see you love pretty things,
flowers, jewelry, and music,
also weapons, and tigers, and lions.
Who are you?
Lady of the brightest light.
Lady of the darkest night.
Who are you?
Warrior?
Mother?
Both?
You've looked into my soul
and gently sealed
the split between the shadow
and the self
seamlessly.
I look to you and see who I might be.

26 Knot So Fast

There is a knot in my stomach.

There is a knot in my stomach the doctor says is purely psychological.

She and I both agree that she can feel the knot in my stomach that she says is not there.

She says, *"Pain, like light, is both wave and particle."*

"Ah, it's pain, and not a knot I gather."

She says, *"It really is a hairball-like thing made of stuff and memories."*

"Seriously? Memories? In my stomach?"

"Yes, seriously," she says.

She says, *"With each passing day more sediment, okay, sentiment, attaches itself to it,*

like a slowly moving something in a bog where nothing goes nowhere fast.

With time it has developed an identity, an aura, a carbon footprint all of its own."

Now that's stretching it I think and laugh, and my doctor laughs with me.

"Here," she says, *"this will help you sleep and forget for a while about the naughty knot.*

It'll put some psychological distance between the pair of you, you've become unhealthily paired.

And this here will ease the pain by freezing the shared memories between you and that knot.

Layer by gross stinky organic layer you will dissolve the knot.

Photon upon photon upon photon it will leave your body each day.

Some nights it'll keep you awake, and some days you'll sleep like a baby.

There's no telling what that scar tissue will do to you."

"Scar tissue? Why didn't you say so before?"

"Well, it's complicated you see, not quite tissue, but it has come from a scarring of the senses, perhaps the sensibilities, probably

both, so work with it, work it, until it is raw, supple, and painful.

I mean, healing, birthing wholesomeness, restoring proper function, and you be the doula."

"How long is that going to take?" I ask.

"Nobody knows," she says. *"Like babies, wholesomeness arrives on its own schedule.*

You keep the baby and ditch the placenta and the umbilical cord."

"And the bathwater?" I ask, facetiously.

27 Kiss My Tiara

I am not
the titular head
of a banana republic.
I am the republic.

28 Antarctica

She's an island far away, cold, remote, uninhabited.
Yet, every government sends it's PhDs
to carve out a piece of the island,
to stake a future claim on her,
all under the guise of science and "testing.
Think again.

29 Metaphorically Speaking

She was a sparkling aqueduct to his parched desert soul.
She was two roasted Cornish hens to his hungry eyes.
Betwixt the camel and her, she was the prettier one.
Their date was sweet as the Medjool dates from Costco.

Peace became her like moonlight becomes the moon, reverse engineered.
Her smile was 500 mg of store-brand paracetamol for his feverish imagination.
It helped, but not a whole lot. His imagination was hotter than the desert in June.
He was a shipwreck on an island in a mirage in a desert that never was.

30 Blackout

The way the social power grid is laid out,
if you've cultivated an inner light,
lights get put out in every room you walk into,
until you start going blind.
Then light is coming out of your eyes
to light your way.

Then come the blindfolds.
When that stops working,
comes the bag over the head.

The straight dope -
You can't get sick enough to make one person feel better.
You can't get dumb enough to make one person feel smarter.
You can't get ugly enough to make one person feel beautiful.
You can't get humble enough to make one person feel gracious.

So quit it!
Quit hiding your light under a bushel.
Quit selling out.
Quit deflecting honor.

You were put on this planet for a reason.
If some think you're here for a season,
you don't have to please them.

Opt out of the darkness.
Walk into the light.
It's been waiting for you a long time.

31 Freedom

I walked in a field bejeweled with wildflowers.
It was a dream
of soft sunshine, warm haze, and pretty breezes.

An arched chevron of little black things took wing.
A hundred birds had left my corporeal being and flown away,
up into the hazy blue.

Little gray specks, invisible now,
they were really shards of shame, blame, and upset
that had never had belonged to me anyway.

And again, I see them,
they've returned,
little swallows with graceful feathers.

Hungry for bugs,
they live now their natural lives.
I live too.
No more a human cage.

32 The Consummate Artist

The air dipped a brush into the dark blue lake
and began painting the sky.
Beginning in the east,
strokes going westward,
when accidentally,
it touched the sinking sun,
and spilled a little of its tangerine
into the thinning inkiness of the west.

From the pewter of yesterday's moon,
it cast on the canvas a minuscule drop of silver
that winked,
growing stronger each minute.
Then came another,
and another,
'nother,
a growing population.

Now I wait
for a silver sickle
grown since yesterday,
for I know
the air is only pretending to paint,
'coz I play along.

This charade goes on
irrespective of you or me,
or what we believe,
or choose to disbelieve.

33 Wide Awake

All neurons firing.
Unusual clarity of comprehension.
All faculties working in unison.
Full throttle living.
Peace within.
Peace without.

xxviii. Digital Art by Shounak Tewarie (Tewarie ©)

34 Durga

This was a poem written as a response to a painting by Andy Warhol from his Rorschach series.

xxix. A painting by Andy Warhol from his Rorschach series (Warhol©, 1984)

DURGA

That's Maa.
You'd better take her seriously now.
She's mad right now.
See those hands on hips?
The glowering eyes?
Yes, she's talking to you.
Look, even the tiger is looking at you.
And don't miss the carcasses of deadbeat asuras
strewn on the ground either.

xxx. DURGA (Illustrated By Jahin Hasin Nishi) (Nishi@, Durga, 2024)

xxxi.* SARASWATI *(Illustrated By Jahin Hasin Nishi) (Nishi©, Saraswati, 2024)

35 Saraswati

Goddess of music, dance, and knowledge,
graceful beyond belief.
She flows like a river
purifying everything she touches.

She saved humanity once,
rolling the world set on fire
into the ocean.

We couldn't save you Ma,
when you were very young,
but trust me, now we'll protect you.

xxxii. Traditional Calendar Art, artist unknown (VISHNU and LAKSHMI)

36 Mahalakshmi

Lokkhi mei
Every baby girl is told, or ought to be told,
she is an incarnation of goddess Lakshmi,
she brings prosperity and good fortune wherever she goes.
Little girls, in a world consumed by appearances,
yearn to be the pretty goddess Lakshmi,
in a pink sari, jewels in her hair,
completely missing the point,
on account of youthful ignorance.

We never tell little children about Alakshmi Ma,
Lokhhi Ma's evil twin,
so we never prepare the young for what might come,
when we begin to prepare to welcome Ma into our lives.
It's only the savviest of parents who educate the young
on the proper rituals for the occasion,
for Alakshmi Ma will be very upset
at the feast you prepare for her more popular sister,
especially if you act like she, Alakshmi Ma, does not even exist,
and don't prepare for her visit.
It's quite possible you have never heard of her,
and obviously don't even know her name.

Alakshmi Ma is a humbling force that deserves a place in every heart,
but she isn't a very popular guest.
Respect her while she stays with you,
accept her into your home with all humility,
offer her the seat of honor at your table.

Look around and see the bounty of Lakshmi Ma's blessings.
Bow to her sister Alakshmi as well,
and she will leave when shown due respect.
Ma will preside as Mahalakshmi.

xxxiii. Traditional calendar art (TRIDEVI)

37 Tridevi

A mother's work is never done.
When you see a mother struggling to keep up,
lend her a hand.
She could benefit from having several arms
like the goddesses but she doesn't, she has just a pair.
If she did,
she'd have her ironing, cooking, homework help,
all done at once.
She could sit peacefully on a lovely lotus,
fragrant and chill,
for over half the day,
instead of running in circles,
picking up after the kids,
dealing with car warranty salesmen from India on the phone,
adding up pennies at the end of the month.

Tell the harried woman she's doing a good job.
She's Ma Saraswati teaching her kids.
Tell her she's Ma Lakshmi making the money stretch.

Tell her she's Ma Parvati, handling everything that gets thrown at her
with a vast spectrum of appropriate responses,
from docile as Ma Gauri to assertive as Ma Kali

She should take heart, pat herself on the back,
give herself some credit for being so responsible,
that she turned into Tridevi Ma,
while she barely had a clue what was going on.

We cannot always be there for our own mothers as helpers,
so find the mother nearest you and tell her she's doing a good job,
and lend her a hand.

Midnight Train to Dorkistan

"… There used to be a graying tower alone on the sea You became the light on the dark side of me…"
(Kiss From a Rose, by Seal)

1 This is The Final Day of Years of Sweetness

Through the fog, he sees a face, two-dimensional, incomplete,
a barely there portrait of a young lady in black and white,
and his imagination fills in the rest of the sketch.

The wind picks up and blows the picture away.
He looks for it everywhere, desperately seeking the image for years,
until one day, he sees her holding the now-tattered piece of paper,
looking closely at it, smiling, shaking her head.
He hears her speak for the first time.

He listens to her speaking on subjects like the weather, politics,
gardening, children, pets, nuclear warfare, chocolate …

*"The woman has attitude, she has a mind, a history, a philosophy,
and a completely distorted sense of reality"* he says.

She says, *"This is me, and that's a really old picture of me,"*
as she walks away.

2 A Perfect Waste of Time

He wished he had had a perfect childhood,
which doesn't exist.

He dreamed up a perfect romance,
which doesn't exist,

with a perfect wife,
who doesn't exist.

He wished for a perfect home,
which doesn't exist.

He longed for a perfect family,
which doesn't exist.

He dreamed of a perfect life,
which doesn't exist.

um... you know how this goes …

3 Jenny of All Trades

The phone rings in my sparse office, an old rotary.
Ring, ring
I answer, *"Marionette Repair Inc. How may I direct your call?"*

A lady with a soft raspy voice replies, *"I am so distraught. Can you help me?"*

"Yes ma'am, I can, I make a living out of it.
Tell me what I can do for you."

"You see, I have an expensive marionette my mother procured for me,
and it is broken."

"Is it the strings, or the crossbars, or the marionette himself?

"How did you know it is a he?"

"Elementary, my dear Watson.
You regard this as a business matter, not a matter of the heart.
Were it a she marionette, a child's doll, one that a mama had procured for her daughter, you would've been crying, not
speaking in hushed tones to a stranger
who works out of a hovel in a dark alley across the tracks at the edge of town."

"Hmmm... I'm dealing with a lowlife, eh?"

"Nope, madam. Well perhaps yes,
if you consider marionette repair a lowly profession."

"Well, how can I get the marionette to you so you can fix him?"

"Fix him?
Well, for that, there's Hillary down the street.
I _repair_ *marionettes."*

" Hehehehe .....funny girl, he's wooden."

"Aren't they all? Brethren of Pinocchio.
I'm just the Blue Fairy and I have Jiminy for an assistant."

"The marionette is broken.
Fix him!
My men will deliver him to you in about eight days.
I trust you."

Click.

I look out the one sliver of glass high on the wall that serves as a window in my little room.
The sun is shining.
The leaves on the tree outside throw pretty shadows across the ceiling.
A patch of the bluest sky peeks into my dark quarters.
The traffic hums along as usual.
The clock ticks quietly, and so does my heart.
All's well with the world and yours truly.

Ring, ring

It's the old rotary.

Something tells me the caller isn't looking for a marionette repair service.
Maybe it was Jiminy or a fellow fairy kin who whispered in my ear, *"Be careful."*

I instinctively use my other identity as I answer politely,
"Faberge Interiors Inc. How may I direct your call?"

A concerned but polite soprano replies,
"Ah, yes, my wife would like some redecorating around the house and pool.
Can you help?"

"Sure," I say,
"Your wish is my command.
We work seven days a week.
We're fairies and elves who do your bidding.
We take no breaks for sleep or leisure or food."

"Well," he says, embarrassed and confused.
"All I had in mind was a little splurge,
for a little more class in the living room,
a little more comfort in the dining room,
and better conversation in the master bedroom.
Can you arrange a makeover?"

"Jeez geezer, who do you think I am?
Aladdin's genie?
Only he can give you a castle and throw in a princess for free.
I work solely to decorate your space.
I love beautifying bare walls and artfully cluttering lonely shelving systems.
That's my forte."

"Name your price."

"For that, we must work on the square footage, and styles of fabric, paint, wood, tile..."

"No wait, it's the ambience I crave.
I've seen your blog.
Give me your best.
I love the sparseness of your Lincoln collection,
the richness of your French collection,
also, the grandeur of your Arthur collection.
Can you give me your all?"

"We're talking major commitment here.
Let's see, I'm busy until February,
then there's the Pixie convention I go to every year.
I can start in March."

"No darlin' you don't understand.
I want it now."

"Let me see.
There's a lady sending over her broken marionette this week."

"(Gulp) ...Er, yes, that, oh, perhaps you didn't know, that was my wife."

"Haaaa haaaaa haaa haaaa...
I see what is going on here.
I've dealt with crazy before but this is the funniest crazy I've ever seen.
I will be awfully busy for the next few months.
Call me when you've made some progress on your own.
Redecorating isn't rocket science,
you just have to become a real boy first, and your minder is another story.
I wish you luck until we meet again."

Click.

It's time again to take the trash out,
to get the mail in,
to walk the dog,
to toss out the kitty litter,
to boil the potatoes,
to go on with life ....

4 Desirée

Desire is an impetuous bitch.
She comes on strong, sudden, forceful, cocksure,
and then she leaves just as suddenly.

Desire is a fickle wench, butt ugly as can be.
Just as he has found love with his missus,
he wants his bald-headed big-boned employee.

A two-faced thief of pleasure she is.
That bitch, that thing, that nothing that she is,
that never leaves except it seems for a quick pee.

Satisfaction is her enemy,
anathema if you will,
like light and darkness presumably.

You could go fifteen years without seeing her face.
When you've just about forgotten what she looks like,
she shows up in two places at once, unexpectedly.

You're embarrassed and all and confused as s#!+.
You say,*" Where have the pair of you been all my life?
Actually, lately?"*

They say," We *heard on the grapevine,
you said you'd do a threesome,
if it were you, Brad Pitt, and George Clooney."*

You go, *"Aww, you're so sweet,
but I'm busy tonight.
You two go on without me."*

It pours when it rains, they say,
and they are right you know,
when you get asked to the lesbo ball shortly.

Have I been living under a rock?
No really, have I?
Or have the birds and the bees gone crazy?

5 Go Set a Watchman

The cat on the hot tin roof couldn't be any hotter.
The trotters are ablaze, especially the hoof pads.

The arch of the back tells you she's ready to spring.
The eyes are ready to pop out of its pretty little skull.

A whole line of boys has been watching over the fence,
trying to predict which way she'll jump, and wagering on it.

The roof's high even for one with nine lives.
There's no safety in jumping onto concrete or into the cactus patch.

She's no fool to put herself in peril so she yowls.
She wails like there's no tomorrow, and maybe there isn't.

They'd be better off going to Vegas with their pennies, those boys.
Besides, what happens in Vegas, stays in Vegas, so there ...

But what happens here is a subject for lengthy discussions
for generations to come in our little town with no name.

6 Dorkius Maximus

I Need a Trench Coat

terrible weather
I feel lumpen and gloomy
it's raining cats'n dorks

Call the CDC

indorktrination
communicable disease
spreads through three nations

Alien Planet

we need to talk 'bout
the alienation crisis
it's bad in Dorkistan

Old School

The Dork Whisperer
dorkumentation specialist
works hard paid little

First Aid

What's a dorkiquette?
band-aid over dork's mouth to
stem flow of dorkiness

The Kingdom of Dork

Dorkius Maximus
a dork so dorky he has
his own genus and phylum

Revelations

when he thinks no one
will ever find out his secret
closet dork speaks

Mum's the Word

I don't talk to dorks
they speak no English
I speak no Dorkistani

New Moon

Count Dorkula said,
"You were extending your neck"
he's so not Edward

Dinner Gong

Dorkalicious is here
bring out the good silverware
he's a delish dork.

7 Oxymorons

When the eulogy has died upon the lips of the weary,
when the tears have watered the gravestone and failed to wet it,
when the spirit has dimmed to its last scintilla,
an invisible light, an oxymoron, comes along to light the way.

8 Hunky Dory

Hunky Dory went walking down the oft-taken road of indecision,
and met with a wall standing smack across it.
Must've been where Humpty Dumpty lost his marbles,
or was pushed, or whatever,
when all the king's men couldn't put him together again,
but Hunky Dory had no inkling of that story,
so he shimmied up that wall, singing a song,
until along came a bohemian girl,
a brown curl peeking beneath her bandana,
bells and whistles on her bodice,
chewing a stick of licorice.
She said, *"Hiya."*
He said, *"Hi ya,"*
not wanting to look like an out-of-towner.
"You look new around these parts.
Want me to show you around?"
tartly she asked.
"Sure," he said.
He jumped off the wall,
and followed her around,
until it was dark,
and she said, *"You've been a bad boy.*
You've been a bad, bad boy.
Come let me teach you a lesson."
He felt a frisson.
The graze of the cold tip of a whip
had touched his hip,
and he felt alive, awake,
in a whole new dimension.
No one, save his mom,
had ever lavished so much attention on him,
or cared to discipline him exactly so.
He felt cared for, protected, loved, young,
and safe in the knowledge he could
indefinitely postpone growing up.
But like all things, this grows too old,
too soon, too bold, too cold, too quickly.
Sickly,
he tried to get away.

9 Hunky Dorian and the Gray Lady

Hunky Dorian got off the plane.
The honeymoon was over.
He opened the door to the limousine
to let his wife in and get in beside her.

As they drove over Brooklyn Bridge,
she devolved like something overlooked in the fridge.
He changed too, like he'd been dipped in an age-defying elixir,
while she turned outwardly gray in demeanor.

They were back in their brownstone four suitcases in all,
the mementos from Barbados were flung to the wall.
They looked one another in the eye,
she was bold, he was shy.

She grabbed him by the collar and kissed him.
She said the flight had been too long and she'd missed him.
They turned the corner into the bedroom,
she turned on the lights, he turned off the gloom.

He spilled some sand from his shoes onto the carpet.
Their roles in their marriage had already been set,
she was to be a picture on the wall,
all eyes and ears, mean and tall,

a Medusa who froze everything with her gaze,
a man, a boy, a brook, even the rose in a vase.
He was to be the eternal boy,
sweet and abiding, naughty and coy.

And so, they lived on, happily together.
She went grayer each year like heather.
He remained youthful forever.

10 Maxim Dorky

Maxim Dorky, oh so lithe and sporty,
graying at the temples, a little over forty,
always at a party looking hale and hearty.

Seated beside his harpy,
who's at the top of his hierarchy,
he's eyeing this young floozy,
who's had a little too much boozy.
His wife is right beside him,
droopy eyelids red around the rim,
downcast lips downright grim.

The lights are low, the music dim.
He walks up to the girl and fills her cup to the brim.
He looks into her eyes and gives her his pseudonym.
He looks a lot like a man who knows he's about to sin.
He looks half apologetically at the harpy who gives him a reptilian grin.
So here we are at the two ends of the room,
a story playing out exactly as it has umpteen times before I presume,
the wife looking on like she's been embalmed, and four weeks in a tomb.
She knows this play-by-play and has blessed this all the way, I assume.
I'm intrigued, in the meantime, by her outlandish costume.
It's Easter today, not Halloween, unless we're doomed.
I'd have thought a wife would fret and fume,
but nope, she's sipping her vodka and gathering more legroom,
while Maxim's oozing charm and slathering it all over the girl.
The girl looks like she's feeling woozy as she gives her bangs a twirl.
I'm watching Mrs. Dorky across the room arranging paper napkins in a whorl.
Maxim stops being his usual "folded in three layers" self and like a proud new flag unfurls.
He leans in, says something to the girl, who laughs too much, too quickly.
He looks across the room in the harpy's direction hopefully.

She's given up, Mrs. Dorky, it seems to me.
She's wearing combat boots, a moleskin shirt, and dungarees.
You're almost grateful she's got no makeup on at all,
because if she had put some foundation on it would have been her biggest pitfall.

The scene across the room has altered in the interim.
The girl has perhaps figured out Dorky isn't single, he's just being gamesome.
She left through the front door, dizzy and sozzled.
Mrs. Dorky shot after the girl while we looked on, puzzled.
Dorky looked shifty, stoic, assured of victory, but a bit like a pyrotechnic display that had fizzled.
His harpy returned, her head held high, and her nose looking even more chiseled.
She waved a pale pink business card ahead of his nose for a whole minute before she gave it to him.
She most likely had imagined he'd be thrilled but he looked like a less than delighted Maxim.
He gave her a peck on the cheek and said, *"Darlin', you shouldn't have."*
No one knew how to remedy this situation, there seemed to be no band-aid for this, nor salve.
Harpy smiled, looked Dorky in the eye, and tousled his hair.
She said, *"You have no idea how much I care about you, teddy bear.*
I know you can do nothing without me."
"Yes dear," said Dorky sheepishly.

We are weirded out by the strange goings-on.
The harpy is happy, Maxim's all forlorn.
She's less of a mystery to most of us, since she's always had the tongue of an adder.
What really does this man want, we wonder.

11 Georgie Porgie

Georgie Porgie and his witchy wifey live down the street from me.
Wifey is fifteen years older than him and a whole lot manlier than he.

Witchy wifey has a pedigree.
Georgie has a college degree.

Georgie's mommy lives across the street from me.
She has a beau about the same age as me.

Georgie's wifey has a lot of money.
Georgie works for a downtown attorney.

Now Georgie knows what he's doing you see.
His Daddy went MIA when he was three.

He modeled his life after his stepdaddy's subsequently.
So, when Georgie goes out of town he's a-spending money on other cuties.

When he's done with work there, he's back to his homies,
where he hides beneath their skirts when the cuties come for their alimonies.

Wifey screams, his mama screams, at the cuties, and Georgie is happy as can be.
The cuties vamoose, and Georgie takes wifey and their kid to the park like a good lil' daddy.

12 The Obedience School Dropout

The witch has a three-headed dog.
She picked out the best of the litter,
handed the breeder some glitter,
and took him away to her home in the woods.

Being three-headed was not a bad thing really.
It simply meant he was three times as smart,
and three times more alert than the regular dog,
what with three brains, six eyes, and six ears.
In other regions of the world
only the gods have three heads,
and are said to rule the three worlds.

Astute as she was, she understood this very well,
but she raised him to become an attack dog,
not just to protect her,
but to attack on command,
without conscience or even rational thought.
Over time he became a harbinger of ruin
everywhere she took him.

Everywhere she goes,
he stays by her side,
and obeys her every command.
Not because he loves her, no baby no,
he just hates himself too much
to trust himself enough
to take charge of his own destiny.
So, he does what she commands him to,
kill the young, scare the elderly,
whatever.

The less he favors himself,
the more he doubts his own judgment,
the more power she gains over him.
She sets him up for failure,
and she can, easily,
because all he does now is attack.
Without thinking,

he makes the mistakes she wants him to make.
She waits for him to begin licking his wounds,
and sprinkles a sparkly powder on them wounds.

She speaks softly and asks,
"Is the medicine working my big doggie woggie?"
knowing all the while it is just arsenic and salt.
She throws him a bone
a few hours after dinner time has come and gone.
Master and dog are as happy as they are ever going to be.

The only thing that soothes the soul of the beast is music,
lyrical, intense, intelligent, beautiful music,
through the spring, summer, and early fall of his years.

As the post-harvest chill begins to settle into his bones,
and he's baying at the moon,
he hears the ♫*hounds of winter*♫ calling to him,
"Come away with us."

The thrill of the hunt puts a blunt on the cold.
He knows the woods better than before.
He trusts his senses more than ever before.

He's gone as fast as he can,
running with the hare,
hunting with the hounds,
not any more of a beast than you or I.

13 Nina

Nina entered the room.

That moment in time became a fulcrum for the timeline of his entire life.
Everything was either 'Before Nina' or 'After Nina.'
Not that Nina had orchestrated this event or even wished it were so,
but she knew he saw her as his savior.

Saviors get crucified, well almost always,
and she wasn't happy with that observation.

She felt like Christ bearing a cross on his way to his own crucifixion,
what with the precedent of everything becoming BC and AD.
the minute folks saw him as a savior.

Saviors often come in pairs,
like the crazy cat lady and her rescue.
Nobody actually knows who rescued whom.

Just everybody and their mom knows saviors are crucified,
routinely and often.
The world likes to embalm them in a moment of superhuman sacrifice,
and then never find out they were merely flesh and blood,
ordinary people who made an extraordinary decision,
and found the courage to follow through,
and just perhaps that Fate stepped in to help.

14 Release

She sees me for who I am,
she sees me naked and whole.
She has looked into those corners of my soul
I knew nothing of before.

Who is she,
and where did she come from?
Is she a friend?
Is she a foe?

Is she a whore,
a charming Trojan,
sent by the enemy,
to destroy my home?

This warmth that rises
in my cooling blood
is a liqueur made of
sunshine, moonshine, starshine, and more.

Who is this witch
with the magic spell
that set me free,
a prisoner in a candy store?

Who gave her permission to remove the dust covers
placed over the treasures of my soul,
so now, when I call her name,
it echoes my own?

She left me with a golden key
to a new universe, but no map of it,
no laws of physics,
no passport,
no address book,
no ticket,
to see me past these familiar shores.

15 Genghis

Never have I seen a human trait cross cultural borders
as does The Genghis Khan Complex.

I am not entirely sure it's in the DSM,
but it really ought to be.

Never have I seen as much unnecessary upheaval
as that triggered by The Genghis Khan Complex.

We should be looking to identifying and isolating
the gene that leads to so much mayhem.

The world can hardly wait to recover from it.

16 ♫ You Only Live Twice ♫

She was Miss Moneypenny to his Bond.
She held the keys to his money box,
and she spoke to the powers that be,
like the one in charge of everything was she.

One at a time, each little item on his annual itinerary,
somehow or another, came under her sole authority,
until a dozen years or so later, he realized,
he had been bound with invisible ties.

Now, a lot of jokes were being made at his expense,
but he never really got them, he'd become so dense.
He had no earthly idea his shirt, his tie, his earth, his sky,
not being of his choosing, had caused him slowly to die.

Bit by bit he had given away his simple pleasures,
his golf cart and fishing rod that had been his treasures.
He looked in the mirror and a stranger was staring back at him.
"Dude, have you seen Sam?" ♫ *the man in the mirror* ♫ asked him.

C-R-A-C-K went the mirror, and he stepped through the broken glass.
No one had told him there was an invisible world out there with no mass.
The neutrons, electrons, all behaved rather oddly,
and he, in turn, began to behave rather badly.

And that was how he came to be known as the Horny Toad.

17 Samantha Was

Samantha was a very good girl.
A very good girl Samantha was.
An obedient daughter,
an exemplary citizen,
a near-perfect girlfriend,
except, she wasn't.

She didn't quite know what it was,
or wasn't,
that made her only an almost good girl,
but not quite good enough, yet.
That was her perfect imperfection.

Her first boyfriend called her a sheep,
but she'd never bleated in her life,
and she was beetroot red not white.
She laughed nervously, *"Really??"*
blushing profusely.
Never did he shield her from his boss' roving eye,
nor from her boss' roving eye.
"Wait, what?" she thought to herself,
"This relationship isn't working anymore."
She packed and moved to her father's apartment,
on the other side of town,
from Staten Island to Manhattan.
Mum's was too far in Connecticut,
and it messed up her accent all over again,
making wide swings back and forth,
between Kiwi and American,
interspersed with minor wobbles,
between Jersey and Central Park South.

Samantha was a social contortionist,
and ever more an emotional quick-change artist.
She was so good at empathy,
she could console a nun for her sacrifices,
and the Devil for his questionable disposition,
in the same breath.
She was a good, good girl,
except, maybe, she wasn't.

Along came a spider and sat down beside her,
and said, *"Are you sure you're not trans?"*
Her eyes popped out of her crimson face.
"I don't believe I am. Why?"
"You are trans. You should dress like a man," he said.
and he crawled away.
Samantha was a very good girl,
so she said nothing at all.

Little Jack Horner sat in a corner and called out to her,
"Sam, Sammy, hey Sexy, don't let anybody put words in your mouth."
Samantha, who was a very good girl, said, *"Aye,"*
and left the building, seething with rage,
"I've watched this movie before.
Why do I even bother feeling any emotion?
Well, I suppose rage is a legitimate feeling.
I'm skipping a step here though.
I revert to the embarrassment
at a personal affront,
startle at a personal boundary being broken,
locked in a stupid loop of
affront, rage, red-faced silence,
affront, rage, red-faced forbearance,
affront, rage, forced red-faced grimace-smile …
I know now to expect that.
Every time I turn around,
boom, a projection, on the blank wall that I am.
I'm not nice, I'm stupid.
I'm a dumb blank wall.
People put a nail on a blank wall
and hang pictures on it."
That was her little treatise on *Projection*.

And so, Samantha became the good girl
who expanded her vocabulary,
and her emotional range,
and lived happily ever after.

18 Goodbye Sam

I was waiting for my son outside the barbershop
on a damp but sunny morning in April.
We'd had a round of April showers that bring May flowers
to our neck of the woods.
Dewdrops hung from the stop sign next to me,
prismatic in the morning sun.
I wish my son wouldn't get haircuts in the mornings before school,
but that's his choice.
And I am his almost-was-a-Boomer mother
who has no choice but to humor him
in a world that has subordinated parents to the youth with a simple phrase,
"Hashtag Okay, Boomer."

So, here I was, catching up on the news outdoors after five months of winter.
The newsprint actually looks different in sunlight.
You know, the paper is yellower, and the print is a different shade of black than it is indoors.
It's the same old doom, and gloom, and Washington gridlock on the front page,
but I can hear the traffic, and birds, yes birds, and people,
and that changes everything.
Instead of getting sucked into Front Page Drama, I'm like, *"Whatever..."*

Something glittery had caught my eye,
I looked up from my compulsive reading,
and there she was,
Sam!
I hadn't seen her all year.
She'd been busy with her renovation project and her new boyfriend,
also clearly needing space to grieve the loss of her brother amid all the newness,
good and bad.
She had even quit the girls' breakfast group and shut down her website,
and here she was, walking purposefully on the opposite sidewalk,
sashaying, I would say, in what looked like a trench coat
with tiny rhinestones all over it.
Nah, those were raindrops not quite dried yet.
She didn't look approachable.
She looked like a woman on a mission,
so I didn't yell hello across the street.
She was lit!
A chandelier.
And that in a plain khaki trench coat, aviator sunglasses, messy hair,

and what looked a pair of low heels in maroon, but I could be mistaken.
Who wears heels on a chilly morning right after it's rained?
Well, Samantha, I suppose.
Then I lost sight of her.

I finished my coffee and my son emerged from the doorway ready to go to school.
We brushed off the hair from his collar and shirt and drove to school,
his breakfast sitting in the drink holder, cold and uninspiring.

I thought of Sam every now and then, wishing I had said hello.
She was always a delight to talk to, smart, cheerful, and informative.
Being in proximity to her *"leveled you up"* no matter how blah your day was.
She had an aura, people said.
I hardly know what that means, maybe it was her personal style.
She always reminds me of the song, ♫ *Singing in the Rain* ♫.

The day went by like any other day,
the week, like any other week,
the month, like any other month.

It was May.
It was time for the gardening club to have its first meeting of the year.
I was really hoping to get the ladies to teach me how to prune and manure hydrangeas.
I wanted pink ones, and blue ones, and purple ones, and white ones.
I heard the trick is in the fertilizer and the annual prune.
I walked in a little late and all I heard was *"Samantha this and Samantha that."*
The girl had quit her job, dumped her boyfriend, sold her apartment,
hitched a U-Haul to her wagon, her wagon to a star, and moved west.
Her only goodbye was a gift of wine and pizza for our first meeting of the year,
and a card with all our names in it, saying she was sorry she left in a hurry,
and would miss us, and that she cherished the good times we had together for five years
before her year of unusual circumstances that pulled her in twenty different directions,
and she had to quit coming to our delightful get-togethers.

We made her a video where we each said a personal goodbye to sweet Sammy girl,
and signed off with a collective, "Goodbye Sam."
Many of us were teary and sad, we hadn't known Samantha had been so dear to us.

19 Men are Dogs

My friend Sam,
short for Samantha
swore she would never marry.
"'Coz all men are dogs," she says.
She did well in her career,
or careers should we say.
She took over her dying brother's startup
and saw it IPO and soar.
Her brother's partner died also,
leaving her his share in the business,
as she had been his only support
through the worst years of his life.

Ms. Mother Teresa is a very kind and strong soul,
and very short on patience for anything that
seems like a waste of energy to her.
So, by her mid-thirties, she stopped dating,
and poured all her energy into her work.
She also taught herself everything she needed to know
about repairing old homes and selling them,
and that's what she did in her spare time.
One house in the valley became her obsession,
an old adobe, whitewashed and festooned with wisterias.
It was the one she wanted to grow old and die in.
So, she fixed it up over the summer and moved in.

There was one catch.
The homeowners had explained to her
they were moving overseas so they had placed
their dog with an adoption service.
The asked if she could take him in if they couldn't find him a home
in the next eight days.
She said okay, never one to turn away a creature in need,
and on the ninth day picked up the big St Bernard *"Arthur"*
and brought him home, to his home really,
since he had lived there the last ten years.
And so, she christened her new home *"Camelot."*
Arthur seemed so forlorn, especially since he drooled so much.
She brought home a Labrador three years old from the shelter.
The lovely Lab was named Felicity

but Sam started to call her *"Guinevere."*
It confused Guinevere at first but she took it in her stride,
blossoming in her new home with all the love shown to her.
The three of them gelled well as summer turned into fall,
playing fetch, going for long walks,
eating together on the patio,
watching *"Sex and The City"* reruns at night.

Right after New Year's Day, as soon as the hullabaloo
of the holiday season suddenly died,
Sam noticed Guinevere had been listless.
She slept all the time and was gaining weight
from refusing to go on walks and playing catch.
And then it hit her.
Guinevere was having puppies,
soon!

A midwife was contacted.
There was new bedding brought in from the store.
A gate had been installed in the kitchen,
so the puppies couldn't wander in.
And the big day arrived.

There were five cute little babies born that night,
sweet as ever, cuddled up against their mommy.
They were all a certain shade of tan,
the exact shade of tan that was the neighbor's Labrador *"Lance."*
"Perhaps," Sam thought, *"I should've just let her be Felicity."*

xxxiv. Multimedia Illustrated by Jahin Hasin Nishi (Nishi ©, Samantha, 2023)

20 The Sleeping Beauty Mines

Much like the famed lost mines
of the revered King Solomon,
The Sleeping Beauty Mines are being picked at
for turquoise of the rarest purity.

The gold mines, they say, have never been found.

I imagine a gold mine filled
with Solomon's wisdom instead,
something so much more useful than gold.

I bring a wheelbarrow, a bucket, a shovel, and a chair.
I don't know why I ♫ *dig dig dig* ♫
but I do it all day long,
digging beneath the platitudes.

Word spreads about the miner
who found *"the gold."*
Maybe she did, maybe she didn't.
We'll see.
So they come in Land Rovers and on dirt bikes,
dressed for the job, or not.
There's as much outback plaid, leather,
and blue jeans out here,
as the camo, the tux, and the Tesla.

It's an honest day's work, mining for gold.
We muscle thieves out of our way as we go.

21 The Curse of the Competent

Here's the problem with being good at what you do,
you are the battleax and the battlefield as well,
and the world is a minefield you are forced to navigate very, very carefully,
even gingerly, if you are a woman.
Remember, you are the battlefield,
your body, your mind, even your soul is a battlefield,
along with your acumen, reputation, your network, your net worth.

It's a lot worse than merely having to tiptoe through the tulips.
This is a life of daily peril to body, mind, and soul,
the only three things you ever actually own in this world.

You don't understand what I am saying here, do you?
Let me illustrate the point with a story.

♫ *There was a man, a lonely man* ♫
He could command a room with his sheer presence,
when he spoke, hearts fluttered,
when he laughed people laughed with him.
He made such a fine figure of a man,
not in the Hollywood leading man sort of way,
but, boy, oh boy
it didn't matter what your type was,
he was your type.

Men greeted him with respect.
The ladies ovulated a little faster when he walked by.

The lady who works the copy machines on the mezzanine
said to me one day, *"I love it when he calls me* ♫ *Senorita*♫.*"*
"Awww," I thought to myself, *"I could pass for a senorita ..."*

My boss's secretary said after the last meeting,
 "Something about him makes me feel like a ♫ *dangerous woman*♫.*"*
My mind went, *"Grrrr ... you nailed it girl."*
Of course, I said nothing, and she is not a mind reader, thankfully.

In his fifty some years on planet Earth
he must've devoted, it seems, a hundred to his craft.
He is remarkable in his ability for solving problems.

Give him a problem, any problem, and it's gone.
Poof! Like magic.
No drama, no fanfare, no protocols,
just sleight of hand and silence.
Damn, he was a study in master-craftsmanship,
and we were taking notes,
copious, detailed, invaluable notes.

The curious detail in this story was,
as far as we could tell by the circulating folklore,
he was always new in town.
And he almost never wore a wedding band.
It appears that he moved frequently,
and was seldom married.
I don't know.
I'm just playing a guessing-game
like everybody else.

As you got to know him
you realized he was a phoenix of sorts,
a resurrection specialist, if you will.
He brought projects, departments, people back to life,
because he knew how refurbishment works.
He told me once his first job was caring for rose shrubs
his father put in planters on their patio.
He didn't have to worry about slugs,
but everything else was a huge problem.
He'd lived all over the world,
solving problems, I presume.

About that fire in his soul,
there is a timeless quality about it,
something that appears to have been carried like a torch
from Olympian to Olympian.

People have worshipped fire for millennia,
agrarian states, Vandal states, theocracies, monarchies, democracies,
everybody honors fire in their own coded ritualistic ways.
Those who succeed the most are those who control it best,
but I digress ...
I'm just not sure about the exact nature of the fire in his soul,
perhaps because it is highly adaptive, dynamic, and evolutionary, like him.

He spoke fluent French, a little Afrikaans,
a smattering of Arabic,
his mother's first language, British English,
his father's first language, Brooklynese,
with equal ease and candor.
He had Hebrew words a-plenty,
and rap music lyrics too.
His language, like himself,
was gloriously multifaceted.

He wasn't religious he said,
but he could tell you the exact book of the Bible
a reference came from.
He could rattle off the names of all the avatars of Lord Vishnu,
in the right order too.
I didn't quiz him on the Celtic and Greek pantheons,
but I'm fairly certain he knows all about Isis and Odin,
and the demigods too.

If you asked him what he did over the weekend,
he'd say he played baseball with the kids in his neighborhood.
His sons were all grown up and moved away
so he volunteered at the local park.

You sensed about him a man who had died,
or a man who was between lives,
perhaps between worlds.
Beneath the cool exterior was a forge.
It appeared he was cooking something in that fire.
No smoke escaped his ears,
but you could tell he was almost done.

And then he found a brand-new job!
He was leaving us to move to Europe.
A "For Sale" sign hung in his yard.
My neighbor was his agent.
Over the three months that his house was on the market,
she got to know him better.

He'd call her every day to ask about the house.
She'd email him every day, but he'd call anyway.
He'd chat for exactly three minutes and say goodbye.
I'm guessing he was multi-tasking,

and the concurrent activity took 180 seconds to complete.
That's what he did at work.
Morning briefings were exactly four minutes long,
desk to coffee machine and back ...
She says she's never worked with anyone before
who can extract and process information
quite as fast he.

She got to know his family a little too.
His brother stopped by for a walk-through
as he was passing through town.
He picked up the mail,
and returned a library book, he said.
His mother called one whole week on his behalf
because he had laryngitis.
My friend says they all made her feel like family
from thousands of miles away,
also while in the same room as her,
a rare quality in people these days.
She got a little teary-eyed.
She'd said her family was getting fractured
over politics and s### lately.

She says she couldn't resist,
even while being happily married,
interviewing his brother for details
on the enigmatic Mr.Just-Moved-Out.
She discovered he was an expert in the fields of
oil refineries, banking, and ballistics.

Lord love a duck!
I had assumed he was a labor relations expert.
He never let on he'd done anything else before,
and we never guessed.

He went wherever life took him, his brother told her,
and never looked back.
He knew he'd simply have to pick up and move
all over again.
He'd build something, an organization, a product, or a system,
and someone with no expertise would come along and lay claim to it,
edging him out ruthlessly.
Everything he'd built would go up in flames

from not being handled with appropriate care.
There was always something that prevented him
from unleashing the sleeping giant within,
money, family obligations, social norms ...

He gave up the sentimentalism of his youth
sometime in his early forties.
His wife grew tired of his aloofness and long absences.
She desired a fixed domicile and roots,
and had wanted it all her life so bad,
she stayed in Texas when he moved here.
The kids were in college and doing well.

"Ah ha! He was married but didn't wear a ring," I said.
"Yes, and no," she said.
His brother told her he had hurt his hand on a rig
so he never wore rings.
He had smiled as he spoke, she says, appearing to be very aware
of the effect his brother has on the ladies.
Frankly, to me, it sounds like the brother was a little too quick
with the alibis regarding the naked ring finger.

Now in Europe,
he had renounced his Dorkistani citizenship,
and settled down in Basel.
A good thing too, timing-wise,
just barely preceding the #metoo movement,
or things might have worked out very differently for him.
He always was one to be the first to detect the minutest change
in anything at all.
If a butterfly flapped its wings in Brazil,
he'd predict the next hurricane headed toward Florida
with approximately eighty-five percent accuracy.
I suppose he had read the winds of change in time.
He was anxious for his wife and sons to join him there.
He said he was getting too old to live alone.
He figured this might be his last big move.

I see a pattern here.
I once had a friend who called it
"The Curse of the Competent."
This was a guy who got shredded to pieces
everywhere he went, eventually.

So he picked up and left, eventually.

It appears that his detractors and competitors
invariably sussed out his weaknesses,
his proverbial Achilles Heel and went for it
roughly between his fourth and fifth year on any job,
which begged the question as to what his shortcomings might be.

Based on what I saw over the five years I worked with him,
they were off-putting but nothing seriously out of the ordinary.
I do believe the flirtations were always consensual and outrageously public.
They did break Biblical laws, not necessarily state and federal laws.
Thus began the nitpicking that spanned every aspect of his life,
work, appearance, kids, home, wife, parents, alma mater…
The enemy sought out his every first, second, and third cousin,
recorded their interviews and asked for family photographs.
The attention was scorching and so destructive,
he found himself staring down the barrel of his gun one night.
But then it doesn't take much to destroy a decent human being.
Death threats, slander, evil paperwork ... anything, will eventually
kill a decent human being.
In the weirdest of ways, he made progress because of it all.
Sadly, however, it's not the happiest of lives that he had had,
because of it all.
I hope in the last decades of his career
people just let him be, let him breathe.
The man is clearly exhausted.
His family is clearly exhausted.
No one should have to pay
such a steep price for excellence.
Yes, we get it, the same fire that gives birth to creativity
burns everyone it touches.

It stokes fires of covetousness, contest, greed, hatred.
It's fire against fire, canceling each other out.
Let's understand combustion and let it not ruin us.
Prometheus gave mankind fire and suffered for it,
let it not destroy us.

Something tells me he's gotten to that exact point in his life,
where he's mastered fire.
Go tell his brother he let the giant within slumber all these years
because he's exceptionally self-aware.
He's studied the Phoenix Dragon within with loving care.
He wasn't about to unleash the beast within
until he had befriended it, earned its trust,
and taught it to sit, fetch, stay, and play dead…

In the middle of my conversation with my realtor friend
I remembered I had no clue what his autograph even meant.
I've had this autograph book since childhood.
I changed many schools as my family moved a lot.
One of my goodbye rituals is to ask my friends and teachers
to write me a note to remember them by.
He wrote something about a graying tower by the sea.
Remind me to look that up …

22 Crucible of Fire

Life will sometime take you
♫ five hundred miles away from home♫
and deposit you into a crucible of fire,
a tinderbox,
a preexisting condition,
that is only just wanting a spark -
you!
You're that one scintilla
of a certain something
that sets off a chain reaction
from a single point of contact,
leading up from the possibility of a smolder,
to a blast heard for miles,
cinder blocks flying through the air,
people running helter-skelter,
emails flying from wrists tired of fielding emails,
you get the picture ...
That, my people, is a foundry for the transmutation of souls.
That is the medium for transactions only known to the angels.
We wring our hands and ask why?
But when has the sphinx ever answered her own riddles?

xxxv. Painting by DEBJIT PAUL (Paul©)

23 A Modern-Day Miracle

Don't ask me to explain because this defies logic,
only hear me out.
In what universe do you witness
a series of unfortunate events proceeding in reverse order?
Now that's a miracle, if you ask me,
but miracles are always suspect.
How would You know, since people are opaque,
that they might have holes in their souls
like some have holes in their soles?
They could walk by you every day and you would never know,
unless you have eyes that can see souls.
Would you notice that they suffer?
Would you offer them solace?
Or perhaps a solution to their problem?
How would you, good citizen, if you didn't even know they were hurting?
So, we come back to the clairvoyance of those who can see souls.
Not many people can.
I can't, I know that for sure.
But those who can, do exist.
I say this not to frighten you,
because, heck, who wants a soul reader in their midst?
I sure wouldn't.
I would feel like I was being stalked all the time!
And so, we come to the bizarrely beautiful conclusion of this story.
Imagine a train wreck that slowly unravels itself.
The train cars put themselves back on the tracks.
The people heal and come back to life.
Their souls and their corporeal selves are back together again.
The holes in their souls seem to have healed too.
For I can see them smiling genuine smiles.
I am almost certain there's an invisible healer of souls and such
somewhere hereabouts.
The engine starts to sputter and hum as it pulls away from you.
Soon it is seen picking up speed,
a horn toots far, far away,
and you wonder if it was all just a dream.

24 Creators of Culture

Whilst we bow before the painter, sculptor, playwright, and newsman,
let us not forget that these are people
who merely reflect what is happening around us.

Whilst we study the happiness index, the crime rate, and the rising seas,
let us not forget there were events within the last hour
that merit your greater attention.

When the little child in third grade came to school and bit his friend,
you might have wanted to check on his family.

That little child said he bit his friend by mistake,
because he felt an unnamable rage rise within,
and in that moment he thought he was a wild dragon.

When you checked on his family
you might have wanted to check on his parents' employer.

He had overheard his parents talking
about something that had happened to his father's boss,
Mrs. P., whose daughter was his best friend from kindergarten,
whom he still met at the park on Sundays at soccer practice.

She had told him that the police had come to her home the previous night.
Her mom had told the police about the bad man she worked for.
Her mother had cried through breakfast and lunch, but she was smiling now.

Her father had driven them all to soccer practice
because her mother's hands were shaking too much,
and that she had been home all week crying.
She had quit her job.
They would have no money for soccer
starting next month.
Her father hadn't spoken at all, all week,
but he kicked the dog every day.
He was looking for a new job too.

The kids sit on a bleacher in silence now,
sharing a bag of mini pretzels,
looking like twins in their matching uniforms,
each with a messy mop of shiny blond hair,
a pair of intense gray eyes each,
and about thirty freckles a piece.

The little boy hadn't bitten the bad man
when he had desperately wanted to.
He hated himself for having bitten his classmate.
His rage remained unresolved.
So, he bit the arm nearest to himself,
his own,
every single day,
and swore he would never have children of his own.

Cultures shift one event at a time.
We create culture as we go about our day.
We add goodness to it,
or we add evil to it,
one decision at a time.

We are creators of culture.

25 You Should Be Writing Horror Stories

Horror stories and Whodunits have always been a staple in every generation.
You should be reading them and writing them too.
Why shouldn't you?
You afraid of a little blood and gore? Huh? 'Fraidy cat??
Suck it up buttercup, and take a seat or a pouf.
Let's enumerate the many reasons you shouldn't leave all the writing to Stephen King.

Take a gander at the morning news,
that's what's happening all around you.
People got shot for nothing on a generic street in a generic town.
A man drowned his kids for insurance and a mistress.
The databases of these many companies were sold on the dark web.
The cops recovered 180 kids from a sex trafficker.
180, not 1, not 10, 180.
A music mogul and his wife were accused of drugging and raping 12 people.

Tell me you want to ignore reality.
Tell me you'd rather watch *The Bachelorette*.
Stop being a glittery little snowflake.
Watch *Dateline* or *House of Cards* instead.

There's fuckery afoot
and you should be talking about it.

Clearly, the sex traffickers selling kids have a business model
that keeps people ignorant or quiet,
and 180 missing children locked in their evil grip.
Clearly, there are thousands of people
who watch these children live every day and do nothing about it.
Clearly, there is technology
to track down the location of these trafficked children
down to the exact 10x12 room they are in.
Write about each child.
That's 180 horror stories right there.
Enough to keep you busy for a year.

The man who drowned his children for an insurance payout,
what's his name?
Where did he go to school?
Who were his neighbors, friends, colleagues, wife, in-laws?
Did the insurance agent smell a rat?
When did the dad come in to buy insurance on his 5-year-old and 13-year-old?
Did he realize there was something going on three years ago
when he got a request for a 250k accidental death insurance on his wife,
something she hadn't asked for?

Here's some parchment and quill.
Get to work.
Share your findings with us.
Let's get to know what is happening in our communities.

26 No Country for False Prophets

Tell me no tale that has no sex in it.
Nobody's buying your story.

Sing me no song that has no gods in it.
We all know who exactly you worship.

So what if you won't name your overlord?
Everybody knows whose arse you're licking.

Please don't pretend money does not matter.
Your economics are plainly apparent to the world.

Tell me no lies,
and you might just be believed.

27 Blindfolds Abound

In the theater of the absurd,
all is possible,
yet all is judged unceasingly.
What brings the actors and the audience together?
I ask myself that question often.
Especially when "cruelty" is mislabeled as "kindness",
and when "healing" is mislabeled as "damage",
and "damage" as "healing."
You really have to shout out loud,
"Stop this circus already!"
Then get out of the building because it's on fire,
for where there are blindfolds there's arson too.

28 Fishes and Loaves

How 'bout 'em Fishes and Loaves?
By the Sea of Galilee, some said it couldn't be done.
Yet you will find that the fishes and loaves
will feed the multitudes,
and the basket holds a little more
to give away
in the hands of a giver.

29 Cheat Codes

That eighth or ninth level,
that unwinnable level,
that every kid hates on his video game quests
is the one you have to win.
Find a cheat code, find a buddy, apply code.
You'll have a better shot at conquering the game.

xxxvi. Samudra Manthan (©, 2020)

30 Samudra Manthan

Tell me now, how does churning an ocean of milk
give you the love of your life, riches, soma, and poison?

It's a product of the vast reserves of courage and guile of the gods.
When something doesn't work, they push through the challenge.

They were unfazed by the sudden appearance of people and objects and crises.
They didn't stop and stare at the jewels and the women.
The poison was dealt with summarily.
They gave us a world where the asuras had been subdued.

31 Shiva's Gaze

The mastery of the Gods
lies not in their power to create or to destroy alone,
but to do both with the same gaze.
That is the transformative power of God's love,
and His wrath.

xxxvii. Painting by Sweta Shrivastava Saxena (Saxena©)

32 Tridev

The Holy Trinity,
Brahma, Vishnu, Shiva,
have had their share of power struggles.
It isn't always the ladies and their catfights,
nor is it the battle of the sexes,
that take center stage permanently.

Much is common between the genders,
even if you don't relate to gender specific conflict,
because they seem so silly
when it's not your gender having a major battle
that you believe
should never have been an issue in the first place.

Brahma the Creator had a head lopped off by Shiva
and he has but one temple to his name
in the whole entire universe.
Vishnu the Preserver
and Shiva the Destroyer
have always been collaborators.
Look at what they gave us,
plenty!
And even kept Brahma on a short tether.

The soul has the same facets as the trinity,
for the gods created us in their own image.
When the Brahma within acts up,
you have to let Shiva's energy take over,
lessen the hubris of the errant one.
Let the Grand Preserver reel in the Creator energy,
subdue the malefic aspects of it all.

Masculine power is a heady mix of jostling energies.
Nothing worth doing in this world can ever be accomplished
without it.
The light and the darkness,
both fully owned, nurtured, judiciously tempered,
in tandem with his shakti,
letting the light cheat a little when it's losing the game,

keeps the world going round.

It hardly matters if you are a man or a woman,
we are all called to discover
The Creator, The Destroyer, and the Preserver within.

xxxviii. Midjourney Creation (Midjourney Creation)

EPILOGUE

Poppies growing among ripening wheat,
rubies red lilting in fields of gold,
Demeter's treasures,
Goddess who fills our breakfast bowls with cereal
and cold milk every morning.

Poppies, the humble corn rose on brown earth
that modern machinery dug into neat rows,
the world lurching from crest to trough to crest,
furrows on Mother Earth's brow.

Poppies on the battlefield
sprung from dragon's blood and soldiers' alike.
Some call them Aphrodite's tears of blood.

Poppies are what you make of them,
rubies, tears, medicine, food, or opium.

It depends on you.

GLOSSARY

I. HUMAN CAPITAL

1. Human Capital - Kans, Krishna's maternal uncle who tried to kill Krishna
2. Movement
3. Colonial Cousins -i) idlis with sambhar, steamed rice and lentil dumplings with a spicy lentil and vegetable soup; ii) kutcheri, carnatic classical music performance; iii) *"Iskander de pooth firangi ho gaye", Urdu for Sikander's progeny have become foreigners*
4. Borderlines
5. It's the Spirit of the Enterprise i) Prithviraj, Indian king from the 1100s ii) Akbar, Indian king from the 1500s
6. Breathe Life Into Me i) Balraam, Krishna's older half brother ii) Gokul, a town in Uttar Pradesh, India, where Krishna spent his childhood
7. The Apprentice
8. Warp & Weft pg 23 1) lyrics from Michael Jackson's "Give in to Me", ♫ quench my desire♫
9. Missing Ingredient
10. The Water Bearer
11. Leaky Cauldron in the Sky
12. Wishing Well
13. Pixel
14. Matchless Wonder
15. What Ails Thee?
16. Force of Nature
17. Thingamajig
18. Quantum Leap
19. Second Banana 1)movie Slumdog Millionaire
20. Rags to Riches
21. The Emancipation Proclamation of the BodyMindSoul 1) Atlas Shrugged by Ayan Rand

II. ANIMA ANIMUS

1. A Thousand Pardons For I Know Not Who I Am
2. Desert Rose
3. The Accidental Cubist - *purdah nashin,* the veiled one
4. The Colors! The Colors!
5. Why Women Should Stay Home 1) Brokeback Mountain 2)Moby Dick
6. The Erroneous Theory of Venus' Envy
7. The Deafening Sound of Silence
8. Cupid's Wet Wings i) Kafka by the Shore and ii) The Windup Bird Chronicles, books by Haruki Murakami, iii) jhaalmuri, Jhalmuri is a popular street snack popular in Bengali, Bihari, Odia cuisines

of the Indian subcontinent, made of puffed rice and an assortment of Indian spices, vegetables, Bombay mix and mustard oil. It is popular in Bangladesh too; iv) ven pongal rice, Pongal is a South Indian and Sri Lankan dish of rice, split yellow mung dal, ghee, cumin, ginger, pepper and curry leaves; v) Gulmohar, a flowering tree with distinctive orange-red blooms, Delonix Regia. Gulmohar is also known as the royal poinciana; vii) dal bhaat, lentil curry and rice, a daily staple in South Asian households; viii) Dida, maternal grandmother of their children, ix) boudi, brother's wife; x) Baba, father

9. More Than Meets The Eye i) *"Hadd ho gayi hai goondagardi ki. Cartoon banake khada kar diya hai shareef logon ko."* It's the limit. They've made cartoons out of respectable people and lined them up; ii) Shakuntala and Dushyanth, myth about a king who married the daughter of a sage and abandoned her having forgotten her married her in accordance with a curse. He sees the wedding ring and recovers his memory; iii)Shakti, literal translation is "power", in this context means the feminine divine; iv) Prakriti, nature, v) Durga, Hindu goddess associated with power, motherhood, protection, wars…; vi) Gauri, literal translation is "fair one", refers to the light skinned and docile version of Goddess Parvati/Kali; vii) ♫ *Hum pe hairaan hai teer Sikandar ka, Hum pe kurbaan hai neel samandar ka* ♫ lyrics from movie Tashan, literal translation, Alexander's arrow is startled by us, the blue hue of the ocean is willing to sacrifice itself for us

10. Why Worry?

11. Microtransactions - i) Zamindar, landholder, ii) Rani, queen iii) Sahiba, honorific for royalty, head of state/estate, fem.; iv) devar, husband's younger brother ; v) Boudi, brother's wife; vi) darwan, gatekeeper or guard; vii) Bundeli, dialect spoken in central India in the region known as Bundelkhand; viii) Dada, older brother ; ix) rasoi, kitchen; x) jhol, a curry with a thin and light gravy ; xi) Dida, maternal grandmother

12. Fault Lines in the Kingdom of Oedipus Rex 1) Desire Under the Elms, play by Eugene Oneil.

13. Where's Electra?

14. Koi Pond

15. Fall Haiku

16. The Awful Simplicity of Ten

III. WHEN WE WERE VERY YOUNG

1. An Alphaby for my Beautiful Dreamer 1)♫ "Baby Mine" ♫ song from Disney movie Dumbo ;

2. Colorlines in the Sandbox

3. The Two Ends of a Telescope dhurrie, handwoven rug, ii) Lyrics from Jonh Lennon's "Woman" ♫ the little child inside the man♫ :

4. Paper Boats on River Time 1)biryani, a rice dish cooked with meats, spices and yogurt

5. Pink Elephants Must Die at Sundown 1) Book The Many Adventures of Winnie the Pooh; 2) The Wild, Wild West, American TV series

6. Happy Pidgin i) howdah, a seat for riding on the back of an elephant or camel, typically with a canopy, accommodating two or more people

7. Fairytalia i) nani, maternal grandmother

8. Hot Mix i) *glucotse biscut ani chaha, cookies and tea; ii)* charmuri, puffed rice iii)sev, thin strands of gram flour, deep-fried and spiced iv)moth, spiced lentil

9. Stranger Danger
10. Here and Now
11. Homesick i) firan, long warm tunic worn in Kashmir; ii) dak bungalow, a posthouse of the old Indian postal service (dak), used as lodging by itinerant British officials and other travelers and as a make-shift courthouse in rural areas
12. Call of the Valley i) Char Chinar, a landmark in Srinagar with four trees, Platanus Orientalis or the oriental plane tree whose leaves resemble the Canadian maple's; ii) wazwan, cooking shop or multi-course meal of Kashmiri cuisine; iii) rogan josh, kashmiri dish of curried lamb in a tomato-based sauce; iv) gushtaba, meatballs in gravy

IV. I WENT TO THE ANIMAL FAIR

1. Splat!
2. Going Somewhere?
3. Furball
4. It's Not Much of a Life Without You 1) Quote from movie "You've Got Mail", "Daisies are the friendliest flowers"
5. "I Want!" Declared the Elephant in the Room
6. Zebra Crossing
7. Swamp 'er Wimp
8. Sans Reflection
9. Protect Your Fur Babies i)the cat's NOT in his cradle, song
10. Pussy Cat

V. EKPHRASI

1. The Dark Side of the Moon 1) Music album by Pink Floyd The Dark Side of the Moon ; 2) lyrics from Hotel California by the Eagles " ♫ on a dark desert highway♫ " 3) lyrics "♫ soul so weary♫ " from "You Raise Me Up" by Brendan Graham / Rolf Loveland ; 4) lyrics "♫ the flip side of the pillow♫ " from the song "You Make Me Smile" by Uncle Cracker ;
2. Starry Night 1) Starry Night, painting by Vincent Van Gogh, 2) "needlepoint of Light and Darkness" quote from "Medelin" poem by Usha Akella ; lyrics "♫ Lucy in the sky with diamonds♫ " by The Beatles
3. Mona Lisa Smile
4. Manipulating Mona
5. Almost David

VI. THE EVOLUTION OF EVE

1. Roses That Grow By The River Juliet
   thank the god of small things 1) lyrics from traditional Christmas carol "Twelve Days of Christmas", "♫ my true love gave to me♫ " ; *you, a river, dragging the ocean behind you."*
2. The Chumpion of Lost Causes
3. Sharmila at Home i) rangoli, hand drawn patterns on the floor
4. The Last Brick

5. Shame) Sita, wife of Lord Ram, she was abducted by King Ravana and was exiled after she passed the purity test by fire

6. Negative Image

7. Filigree as a Fact of Life

8. That Topsy Turvy Feeling

9. Shakuntala i) Shakuntala, the daughter of a sage who married King Dushyanth who abandoned her having forgotten he had married her in accordance with a curse. He sees the wedding ring and recovers his memory

10. Struggle

11. Ode to a New Song

12. Paris

13. Dualism and Beyond

14. Splash 1) Squidward, a character in TV show "Spongebob Squarepants"

15. Creation Destruction Preservation

16. Star Girl 1) "♫ *Starry starry night*♫ " *lyrics from song by Don McClean; 2)* Geometry of Lilies, a collection of essays by Steven Harvey; i) Om Hrim, six pointed star that represents the union of both the masculine and feminine form, more import. ii)Najmat Dawud, seal of Prophet Suleyman, or King Solomon "♫ *Trusssssssssst in me*♫ " *lyrics from Disney movie Jungle Book;*

17. Alice Matter

18. Winter Fallow

19. Humsini i) Bharatanatayam, Indian classical dance form that originated in the state of Tamil Nadu; ii) Kanjivaram saree, six or nine yards in length, pure mulberry silk and are woven with gold or silver lace and motifs, originally woven in Kanchipuram, Tamil Nadu, India

20. Transmutation 1) lyrics from Disney movie Alladin, ♫whole new world♫

21. New Beginnings

22. Persephone's Reprieve

23. Complimentary Angels i) ♫*Beautiful but flighty*♫ *lyrics from song by* Tennessee Ernie Ford

24. Blame it on Her(a)

25. Shadow Play i) Devi, goddess

26. Knot So Fast

27. Kiss My Tiara

28. Antarctica

29. Metaphorically Speaking

30. Blackout

31. Freedom

32. The Consummate Artist

33. Wide Awake

34. Durga i) Durga, goddess of war

35. Saraswati , i) Saraswati, goddess of learning and the arts

36. Mahalakshmi i) Mahalakshmi, goddess of wealth; ii) *Lokkhi,* Lakshmi, *iii) mei,* girl

37. Tridevi i) Tridevi, the three main goddesses in one avatar

VII. MIDNIGHT TRAIN TO DORKISTAN

  1. It's The Final Day of Years of Sweetness

  2. A Perfect Waste of Time

  3. Jenny of All Trades 1) Jiminy, character from the Disney movie Pinocchio

  4. Desiree

  5. Go Set A Watchman

  6. Dorkius Maximus

  7. Oxymorons

  8. Hunky Dory

  9. Hunky Dorian and the Gray Lady

10. Maxim Dorky

11. Georgie Porgie

12. The Obedience School Dropout 1) ♫*hounds of winter*♫ song by Sting

13. Nina

14. Release

15. Genghis

16. You Only Live Twice 1) You Only Live Twice, Bond movie, and song by Leslie Bricusse ; 2) ♫ *the man in the mirror* ♫ *lyrics by Michael Jackson*

17. Samantha Was ♫ *Singing in the Rain*♫ *song by Gene Kelly*

18. Goodbye Sam

19. Men Are Dogs

20. The Sleeping Beauty Mines 1) ♫ *dig dig dig* ♫ *lyrics from Disney movie Snow White*

21. The Curse of the Competent 1) ♫ *Senorita*♫ *lyrics from song by Camilla Cabello* 2) ♫ *dangerous woman*♫" *song by Ariana Grande*

22. Crucible of Fire 1) ♫ *five hundred miles away from home* ♫ song lyrics by Peter, Paul, and Mary

23. A Modern-Day Miracle

24. Creators of Culture

25. You Should Be Writing Horror Stories

26. No Country For False Prophets

27. Blindfolds Abound

28. Fishes and Loaves

29. Cheat Codes

30. Samudra Manthan i) Samudra, ocean ; ii) Manthan, churning; iii) soma, drink of immortality ; iv) asuras, enemies of the gods

31. Shiva's Gaze i) Shiva, god of destruction and regeneration

32. Tridev i) Tridev, the Holy Trinity of Shiva, Vishnu, Brahma

EPILOGUE ♫ Fields of Gold and Barley ♫ song by Sting

ACKNOWLEDGEMENTS

I would like to thank the amazing group of people I found on Fiverr, across the oceans, in six different countries, on three different continents, who turned my manuscript into a book. Magicians, every single one of them! Racheal Daodu of *Accuracy4sure* formatted the book. Jahin Hasin Nishi of Studio ZetaBay painstakingly enhanced my photographs, editing out glare, and patching up old photos. They formatted the frames on some of the artwork. My beta readers, Vanessa Dreme and Jacob Kyden, gave me excellent. Kristiana Reed was my very thorough and punctual editor. Cara of Fluky Fiction did a final proofread. Phew! Lesia at German Creative did the cover and poster, picking out just the right colors for the book. Dani of Cover Creation did a fabulous job with my book description.

My book wouldn't be half as pretty without the gorgeous artwork by many accomplished artists whose paintings illustrate my poems. My grandfather Shri Sukumar Deuskar painted the portrait of my grandmother Romola Deuskar, which accompanies the poem "Here and Now". My friend, and my mom's student in fifth grade, Sweta Saxena painted "Krishna Dancing on Kalia" and "Shiva Nataraja". Shri Pramod Kurlekar's portraits are such a grand addition to the book. Many thanks to Dr. Tejikrishna Walli for permission to include his father Shri Dina Nath Walli's paintings of Kashmir. My utmost gratitude to Gail McCormack, Shri Prafulla Shukla, and Walid Sayed for their permission to include their artwork. Special thanks to my classmate and dear friend Indriyajit Sethi for permission to include his photograph in my book. Fatima's digital portrait of a young lady in a blue veil always gets compliments from everyone who sees it. Thank you for the lovely illustration. Portraits of Samantha and Ashima were done by Jahin Hasin Nishi, skilfully executed in multimedia. Debjit Paul's watercolors are just beautiful. There are artists whose works I have included but haven't heard back from after several attempts to reach them, like Sumita Samant, and Shounak Tewarie, I hope you are okay with me adding your beautiful creations to my book, and if you're not, just let me know. Images that have no artist's signature or copyright on the image have been listed as "Artist Unknown".

Thank you to my parents and teachers who taught me to read, and write, and truly enjoy the written word. My dad opened up for me a world beyond pigtails and frilly frocks, talking to me about human psychology, science, music, military maneuvers, national politics, boxing, painting, sports... My mother was an English teacher, yup, and spelling mistakes and dangling participles were cardinal sins. Thank you, Papa and Mummy, for all the evenings and weekends we spent reading together, singing together, and just shooting the breeze. Many of the topics I write about now are derived from things you said to me on random evenings while we sat in the living room, unwinding after a long day, or sat at the dining table, you with your paperwork, and me doing my homework, sometimes by candlelight, because load shedding was a thing back then.

Thank you to my Nani who decided I was too old to be a nonreader at five and believed I was supposed to be reading Enid Blyton and The Brothers Grimm independently already because she had taught herself to read at three.

I owe a huge debt of gratitude to my teachers and professors who molded my thinking and my writing.

Thank you to my kids, who keep me from growing up too fast. I love looking at the world through your eyes. I am always left speechless by your wisdom.

I guess I owe me, myself, and I some heartfelt gratitude for turning my diary into a book. It wouldn't have happened without early encouragement from friends like Usha and Renu, who saw potential in my writing and told me I should publish it when I was all about keeping my diary a closely guarded secret. Thank you for seeing value in my poems.

My apologies to those I haven't mentioned by name. Thank you for making this project possible. Lakh lakh shukriya!

TABLE OF ILLUSTRATIONS

BIBLIOGRAPHY

(n.d.). Retrieved from http://themisathena.booklikes.com/post/505071/good-night-reblogged-from-woman-reading

(n.d.).India. Retrieved from http://vintageindianclothing.tumblr.com/page/42

(n.d.). Retrieved from https://pin.it/1gIrLFZ

©, D. J. (2020). AYURVED AND CHURNING OF THE OCEAN. *JIVOTPATTI AYURVED.* Retrieved from https://www.jivotpatti.com/blog.html

Deuskar ©, S. (n.d.). India.

Fatima©. (n.d.). Fiverr, Pakistan.

Kurlekar ©, P. (2012). India. Retrieved from https://pnkurlekar.blogspot.com/?fbclid=IwAR3xNGIz3BhEPqKDeToCaPnZO7a8uQNKSFAdrcdGA1rtVVloc7uyorriHwM

Kurlekar ©, P. (2023). *'A classical dancer'.* India. Retrieved from https://www.instagram.com/p/CvmCaVKs6gX/

Kurlekar©, P. (n.d.). India. Retrieved from https://pnkurlekar.blogspot.com/?fbclid=IwAR3xNGIz3BhEPqKDeToCaPnZO7a8uQNKSFAdrcdGA1rtVVloc7uyorriHwM

McCormack ©, G. (n.d.). Australia. Retrieved from http://www.gailmccormack.com/

Nishi ©, J. H. (2023). *Ashima.* Bangladesh. Retrieved from https://www.instagram.com/ryuna_ryu/

Nishi ©, J. H. (2023). *Samantha.* Bangladesh. Retrieved from https://www.instagram.com/ryuna_ryu/

Nishi©, J. H. (2024). *Durga.* Bangladesh. Retrieved from https://www.instagram.com/ryuna_ryu/

Nishi©, J. H. (2024). *Saraswati.* Bangladesh. Retrieved from https://www.instagram.com/ryuna_ryu/

Paul©, D. (n.d.). Jsmshefpur Public School, India. Retrieved from https://www.facebook.com/debjit.paul.10?mibextid=ZbWKwL

PAUL©, D. (n.d.). India. Retrieved from https://www.facebook.com/debjit.paul.10?mibextid=ZbWKwL

Peckler©, Z. (n.d.).

Samant ©, S. (n.d.). India. Retrieved from https://www.facebook.com/profile.php?id=100017273050917&mibextid=ZbWKwL

Saxena©, S. S. (n.d.). India. Retrieved from https://www.facebook.com/sweta.shrivastavasaxena?mibextid=ZbWKwL

Saxena©, S. S. (n.d.). *Krishna.* India. Retrieved from https://www.facebook.com/sweta.shrivastavasaxena?mibextid=ZbWKwL

Sayed ©, W. (n.d.). *Fall.* Italy. Retrieved from https://www.facebook.com/profile.php?id=100063478840940&mibextid=ZbWKwL

Sethi ©, I. (Director). (n.d.). *Gulmohar Tree* [Motion Picture]. Retrieved from https://1.bp.blogspot.com/-mIyPpynlwCA/UWoZWDUXsoI/AAAAAAAAADk/7bdPNcLTGFY/s1600/Gulmohar+courtesy+Indriyajit+Sethi.png

Shukla©, P. (n.d.). *Cricket Match.* India.

Tewarie ©, S. (n.d.). *Shiva*. India. Retrieved from https://www.byshounak.com/

Walli ©, D. N. (1941). *Chinars in Autumn*. Kralapora village, India. Retrieved from
      https://www.facebook.com/DinaNathWalli

Walli ©, D. N. (1946). *Mar canal*. Bohri Kadal, India. Retrieved from
      https://pnkurlekar.blogspot.com/?fbclid=IwAR3xNGIz3BhEPqKDeToCaPnZO7a8uQNKSFAdr
      cdGA1rtVVloc7uyorriHwM

Walli ©, D. N. (1961). *Village Bemuna Kashmir*. colony in Srinagar, India. Retrieved from
      https://www.facebook.com/DinaNathWalli/photos/pb.100063749378643.-
      2207520000/464446363644363/?type=3

Walli ©, D. N. (1967). *A house boat in moonlight*. India. Retrieved from
      https://www.facebook.com/DinaNathWalli/photos/pb.100063749378643.-
      2207520000/464453416976991/?type=3

Warhol©, A. (1984). *Rorschach*. United States. Retrieved from https://whitney.org/collection/works/11284

In THE WRITING DISORDER

Lotophophagi
The Erroneous Theory of Venus' Envy
Why Women Should Stay Home to Raise Their Young
and Why Men Must Not Go Whaling
Coda:
To Morpheus
Negative Image
The Two Ends Of A Telescope
The Emancipation Proclamation Of The BodyMindSoul

In URBAN CONFUSIONS
Shame
Mona Lisa Smile
Manipulating Mona
Kiss My Tiara

In DI-VERSE-CITY
Quantum Leap

In COURAGEOUS CREATIVITY
They say the skies of Lebanon are burning.

In CALLIOPE
Ode to A New Song

In BURNING WORD
The Chumpion of Lost Causes

In PUNK SOUL POET
Roses That Grow by The River Juliet

In ELEPHANT EARS PRESS
"I Want" Declared the Elephant in The Room

In MUSE INDIA, under the pen name Anaamikaa
Cupid's Wet Wings
The Deafening Sound of silence
Darkness to Light
A Thousand Pardons for I Know Not Who I Am

AUTHOR BIO

Sonali Deuskar Gurpur writes fiction and poetry. Her work is informed by her interests and the many roles she plays in life.

Coming Soon…

A DOZEN ROSES-

A DOZEN ROSES is a collection of anecdotes.

Like a bouquet of roses, these anecdotes will brighten your day!

These loosely connected stories are written in the form of fables, jokes, and short stories about four women in an extended family striving to live out the American dream. Suburbia, though, isn't always all it's cracked up to be. These first, second, and third generation immigrants from South Asia will inspire you, bring you to laughter, and to tears.

Their happy and dysfunctional family's foible's are so true to life you're bound to understand their journey and enjoy their experiences.

Published by Z's Publishing Company LLC
For more information, visit zspublishingcompany.com